Gaby Knight

MIKE IN THE MIDDLE

Copyright © 2024 by Gaby Knight

Contact: gknightauthor@gmail.com

Cover Design: Yulia Horobets

Editor: Megan Sanders

ISBN: 979-8-9923934-0-8 (paperback) 979-8-9923934-1-5 (hard cover)
2 1

To my wonderful husband Justin
for his support from first draft to completed novel

And to the real Mackenzie and Rachel

Chapter One

If it was legally mandatory to be best friends forever, Mackenzie Bishop and Rachel Hoyt would be questioning their life choices before graduating high school. But this was far from their minds as they met for the first time at St. Joseph's Catholic High School's cafeteria a few months into the school year. Freshmen Mackenzie and her best friend Serena Moore were looking for an open table during lunch when the latter found her choir friends waving her over. Serena walked up to the table and put her lunch tray down.

"Hey, Rachel, how's it going?" Serena said.

"Hey, Serena," Rachel began. "Help me out here. Everyone else is complaining that hitting C above the staff for five measures is too much."

"Eh, it's kind of hard," Serena said as she turned to Mackenzie. "But anyways, Rachel, this is Mackenzie. We have Algebra and Spanish II together. Mack, this is Rachel. We have choir together and we attended St. Peter's for middle school."

"Well, just eighth grade."

"Yeah."

Serena then ignored her friends in favor of her lunch as they politely greeted each other. Both were ready for her to continue the conversation, but Serena wanted to eat. Serena was a social butterfly who wanted her friends to also become friends.

Noticing Mackenzie's sheet music under the table, Rachel decided to take the initiative.

"So, Mackenzie, I assume you are in band," Rachel started.

"Yep, I'm the trombone first chair," Mackenzie said as she felt a silence fall around her. She didn't realize she blurted it out. "You're a soprano, right? The snobs of the choir section?"

Serena laughed at the comment. Rachel did not.

"I prefer the icing of the choir section," Rachel said.

"One of my older sisters was an alto in her high school choir, so I've heard it both ways. She said the sopranos know they are home when they can't find the key and don't know when to come in," Mackenzie lightly ribbed.

She figured if Serena was chill enough, the rest of her soprano friends would also be good humored. Her friend smirked at that remark in between bites. Rachel stared, frustrated.

"That's not funny," Rachel said point-blank. She then turned to Serena. "Serena, are we still on for homework and going to the opera Saturday? My parents are willing to take us to Bloomingdales to get last-minute dresses."

"Thanks, but I can't go now." Serena sighed. "My grandparents from Michigan are visiting this weekend, so we have plans with them. My grandma fell last year, so we're trying to spend more time with her since her health is degrading."

"Oh," Rachel said. "Okay, I'll get someone else who may be free. I just want to see if these singers will hit their arias correctly. I've seen the Magic Flute so many times that I guess I'm spoiled."

"I'm sure it will be great no matter who you take," Serena said while shoving food into her mouth.

"Yeah, I just hate it when people make mistakes on stage and you can tell," Rachel said. "They practice so hard, and it's almost a letdown to the audience. I don't want to rant to my parents in the back of their BMW this weekend."

Mackenzie tried her best to not roll her eyes during the whole conversation. What teenager enjoys opera? Also, do all private schools have plenty of rich kids who just casually flaunt their wealth?

Mackenzie found herself staring at Rachel, stunned by what she heard. She almost made eye contact with her before inserting her weekend plans.

"I'm staying home this weekend and doing schoolwork," Mackenzie said awkwardly. "Maybe I'll go see a movie."

"Yeah, I feel like Algebra is going to kick my butt Saturday with all the problems Mrs. Chalk gives us," Serena said.

As the lunch bell rang, all three girls got up to exit. Serena, semi-oblivious to the situation, walked to English class with another friend without a concern.

Rachel, feeling self-conscious of what she said and how Mackenzie seemed to stare at her, continued to Honors Chemistry I, walking down the freshly waxed staircase that smelled like cleaner. She passed some other students making pensive faces as they headed to the science hallway, wondering if they were nervous about class or being as awkward as she felt. Did she say something out of line?

Mackenzie rolled her eyes as soon as she was out of sight of Rachel and Serena. What did her friend see in that upper-class jerk?

St. Joseph's Catholic High School stood tall as a ten-year-old, three-story building for higher learning. The college preparatory academy accepted all kinds of Catholic students, rich, poor, geek, jock, serious about faith, and those who needed teachers to remind them to go to confession. This student body of 800 was made up unique individuals. The Dominican Sisters were as friendly as the lay teachers. Mackenzie remembered the class president and vice president telling her during freshman orientation that all walks of life were welcome and the student body was not stuffy like Catholic schools of the past. Was she being pranked?

✼ ✼ ✼

Mackenzie Joan Bishop was number six of eight children in the Bishop household. Her family was super Catholic, including the part where her parents said they practice Natural Family Planning but still ended up with eight children and driving a twelve-passenger van to transport the family everywhere.

Her father, Jacob, worked as a quarry manager at all hours of the day. He didn't make much, but he was able to provide for his family. Because he was busy, he was a bit aloof to his children. Jacob knew his children's names and what schools they attended, but he couldn't name what classes Mackenzie took or who were her friends.

Mackenzie's mother, Julie, was a homemaker and proud of it. In between taking care of the children, she tutored Latin online to pick up some of the family's expenses. She also preferred online education to in-person because she was socially anxious. Mackenzie's mother was fragile after a few breakdowns over her lifetime involving her parents disapproving of her decisions in college and marrying Jacob young.

Mackenzie closed the front door with some extra energy when she got home, accidentally slamming it.

"How was school Esther— Junie— Mary Grace— Mario— I mean Mackenzie!" her mom stumbled through.

"Fine," Mackenzie said before running upstairs.

Mackenzie was used to getting mixed up with all of her siblings' names.

She grew up poor but knew that didn't matter. She only wanted space in her room to listen to music in peace for the moment. But, in general, she desired more attention from her parents. She was ignored due to her older siblings being in grad school, medical school, married with their own children, or being workaholics. Her little siblings stole the rest of the attention, as babies of the family usually do. Who would rather pay attention to a fourteen-year-old than to seven and ten-year-olds?

Still, Mackenzie knew her place and was used to it. While all her siblings stood out with their blonde hair, hers turned dark brown when she was nine. While her siblings got tall, she stood at the average height for her age. While her siblings got top marks and were sports stars or winning art competitions, Mackenzie was a bench warmer on the soccer team. She worked hard to get a spot on the soccer team even though she wasn't on a travel team or looking to play in college. She just liked the sport, even if she didn't keep up with her national team hopeful teammates.

Mackenzie was ready to wash off the day and go to bed after her homework was semi-done. She would wake up early the next day to finish it. As she walked up the stairs, she heard Junie and Mikey, her two youngest siblings, arguing.

"Hey, Junie. Hey, Mikey," she called.

They stopped for a second before yelling back hey.

"Hey, high school girl, shouldn't you be doing homework and slaving away? St. Joseph's students are held to a higher standard than the average saint."

Mackenzie looked up. It was her favorite older sister, Esther, who just got back from college on fall break. Mackenzie squealed and hugged Esther.

"Esther! How are you?" Mackenzie smiled.

"Oh, just sleep deprived but excited to see my favorite sister." Esther smiled.

Esther was Mackenzie's closest sibling, and she couldn't believe her college junior sister decided to spend time with her on her week off instead of going somewhere cool with her college friends.

"How are you, little sis?"

"I'm fine."

"How was your day?"

"It was fine."

"No, really, tell me about your day. Your day wasn't ruined by that troll of a religion teacher, Mr. Murphy, was it?"

Mackenzie laughed.

"No, I just met this girl today who is friends with Serena. She's this total snobby, entitled type. I don't get why Serena is friends with her." Mackenzie sighed.

"That sucks. Maybe you should ask Serena why they're friends," Esther suggested.

"Well, who cares about high school? What's college like? Going out to crazy parties? Getting drunk and booty scoping?"

As soon as Mackenzie said that, Junie opened her door and yelled, "Booty scoping!"

"Please don't tell mom I said that," Mackenzie said in desperation.

"Booty scoping! Booty scoping! Booty scoping!" Junie kept yelling loudly.

Thankfully, their mother called them downstairs to dinner at that moment, which distracted Junie from yelling again.

Chapter Two

The next day, Serena and Mackenzie were sitting at their desks for Spanish before class started. Serena was doodling in her notebook when Mackenzie, still thinking about her awkward conversation with Rachel the day before, poked her friend on the shoulder.

"Hey Serena, what's the deal with Rachel?"

"What do you mean?" Serena looked up.

"Well, why is she the way she is?"

"You mean like awkward?" Serena asked. "Well, she didn't have many friends because her family moved a lot. We met last year at St. Peter's when she transferred, and we were in the school play together."

"Yeah, but what do you like about her? She seemed... snobby."

"As pretentious as she is, she's pretty nice! She's caring and loyal. Last year, she stood by my side when I got bullied by some stupid guys and stuff."

"Okay, but is she really that snooty? Like all she likes is opera and eating caviar?"

"Yeah, she likes opera, but she also listens to Top 40 music. She might have a debutante ball soon, but she'll still wear jeans and t-shirts on the weekends."

"So, do you guys actually watch operas together?"

"Not really," Serena said. "I told her I was interested in seeing one, because why not? It's fine if you guys don't like each other, but trust me, Rachel is a great friend. She's helpful and cool, and while we may not have the same interests, she doesn't seem to care that much. It's just nice to have some friends to sit with at lunch."

Their conversation was interrupted by the sound of the class bell and Señora Brink making everyone stand up to pray.

After Spanish, Mackenzie went to English while Serena found herself in the choir room. She sat with her fellow sopranos, including Rachel. Serena was enjoying listening to her classmates talk about their other classes and how they were going to hit C above the staff when she noticed Rachel staring at her.

"What's up, Rachel?"

"Nothing," Rachel said. "My head hurts from math class."

"I'm sorry, math is hard."

"But how long are your grandparents staying this weekend? Could we still hang out somehow?"

"Grandma and Grandpa Moore are arriving tomorrow night and will stay through Wednesday. I'm sorry, we're just worried about my grandma. She's smart but fragile. She broke her hip last winter."

"So, you still can't make it?"

"No, Rachel, I really can't."

"Okay, I guess I'll find someone else."

Rachel looked down at her sheet music in disappointment and sighed.

"It's not you, I promise," Serena said. "Don't be dramatic."

"I know, I was really looking forward to this event with you," Rachel replied. "I don't know what to do with the extra ticket."

"Extra ticket to where?" mezzo-soprano Kate Parsons asked. Everyone in the section turned toward Rachel.

"I'm going to the opera this weekend in the city if anyone wants to join me."

"What is the show?" piped up Mary Kate Love.

"The Magic Flute," Rachel said. "It's Mozart."

"Sounds like fun! What time Saturday?" Mary Kate said.

"Seven p.m."

"Count me in if you can," Mary Kate said.

"Sounds like a plan." Rachel smiled. "Dress up if you can."

"I'll text you pictures of some dresses after school."

Rachel's smile showed for the rest of class.

✷ ✷ ✷

Rachel Cassandra Sarah Jane Hoyt always felt misunderstood. Although there was nothing wrong with her per se, she always was a bit of an outsider.

The trust fund child of two business executives, Rachel was their miracle baby. Her parents moved a lot before settling in Brightsville, Virginia, and she had never had close friends. By the time she was in sixth grade, she wasn't sure how to hold on to people her age.

Rachel's parents, Edgar and Cynthia, were ten years older than their daughter's classmates' parents. The two enjoyed not having kids for a while but were happy when Rachel arrived. They put all the energy they could into her, knowing she would make them proud in some way. Whatever Rachel asked for, they always delivered. The one thing they couldn't give her was friends her age.

Without any siblings and constantly on the move, Rachel felt her parents were her best friends. Growing up alone, Rachel always felt she was right and was extremely stubborn, even with herself. With every bad test grade, she beat herself up, and in every argument she got into, she was always right.

She was used to moving every other year, so she didn't feel attached to any one place. Going to St. Joseph's after attending St.

Peter's in eighth grade was a new experience for her. She was glad everyone else was new as freshmen.

She never watched whatever the children her age were watching, played with the same toys, or listened to the same music, until Serena introduced her to pop music. She had her parents, and they had always brought up interesting topics such as politics, current events, classic films, and tv shows that were maybe a little too mature for Rachel.

It didn't help that Rachel didn't physically fit in with other girls her age. Standing at five-eleven at fourteen, she was constantly recruited for athletic teams, even though she was clumsy. She was sensitive to sounds like chewing and fingers tapping on desks.

And she never felt nor saw herself as one of the attractive girls at any of her schools. She was okay with that—she compensated with her intelligence and capabilities. By the time she entered high school, she wasn't sure how to relate to other girls if they didn't reach out to her first. Serena became her first close friend when she approached her eating lunch alone and told her no one should be friendless. Rachel sat next to Serena in language arts and religion classes in eighth grade, and the latter always had something nice to say. Sure, Serena wasn't always self-aware, but she always invited Rachel to lunch and after-school events, along with sharing her favorite Top 40 playlists, which she didn't always dislike. Serena even taught Rachel some American Sign Language before she visited the Moore residence and met Serena's deaf father.

Rachel also found friends in the high school's beta club and her honors study groups. She was finally finding her niche.

Rachel's only other friend was her corgi, Orwell. Her parents brought him home when she was nine, after they moved from yet another state. Unlike humans her age, Orwell was easy to talk to and nonjudgmental. The older dog energetically bounded up to her when she got home from school.

"Hi, Orwell, have you been a good boy?" Rachel happily asked the ankle-licking dog.

Orwell jumped up and down and panted happily. Rachel went upstairs to her room and did homework while waiting for her parents to get home. She got lost in thought about Serena rejecting her plans but was glad Mary Kate was currently texting her for style advice.

Later at dinner, her parents asked her about her day and if Serena was ready for the opera.

"Serena's grandparents are in town, and her grandma is ill, I guess." She shrugged. "But I got Mary Kate Love to agree to go. She's also in choir with us."

"Who is Mary Kate?" her father asked.

"She's also a freshman. I think she likes opera. She was just sitting with us at lunch and offered to go. I think she's into music, since she knew who Mozart was."

"We'll have fun with her then." Cynthia smiled. "Does she have a dress?"

Chapter Three

Serena continued her efforts to make her two friends get along during lunch that Monday. She decided to break the ice by asking them about their weekends.

"It was okay," Mackenzie said. "I just did homework while my siblings ran around the house."

"I had a good time at the opera with Mary Kate," Rachel said. "The arias were perfect, but I guess I just feel disenchanted from seeing this musical over and over."

Serena nodded along happily to both stories before silence fell. She decided to bring up her weekend in hopes of restarting the conversation.

"So, my grandparents are still here, but we had fun. My grandma saw two pigeons on our back porch having sex and tried to get my sister and me to watch. My mom was like, 'NO that's gross,' but my grandma was like 'Oh Bunny—her nickname for my mom—it's the circle of life,'" Serena laughed.

Mackenzie looked at her bemused but didn't say anything. Rachel looked like she saw graphic roadkill.

"Why are you telling me this?" Rachel snapped.

"I thought it was funny," Serena said.

"Your grandma is frail and getting old and you just make fun of her with that disgusting story? Seriously, of all the things you probably did with your grandparents this weekend, who you don't often see, this is the most amusing one you want to tell us?" Rachel continued.

"Hey, she thought it was funny," Mackenzie piped up. "I liked it."

Rachel glared at Mackenzie. Why defend this weird story?

"It's fine. My grandma is doing better," Serena said, trying to calm the situation.

At this point, Serena wished her friends could get along in front of her. A second awkward silence took over the group as Serena pretended there was something on her blue and white plaid skirt and picked at nothing. Mackenzie noticed what she was doing and started dusting fake crumbs off her navy uniform sweater. Rachel raked her quinoa with her fork, half furious she had to hear that story and half frustrated at how she reacted and made things weird at the table. After ten minutes of silence, the lunch bell finally rang to break the awkwardness.

✮ ✮ ✮

"Hey Serena, why are you friends with Mackenzie?" Rachel asked her point-blank after school.

"Well, she's pretty nice and we met at orientation." Serena smiled as she packed her books into her backpack.

"But what's her appeal? She seems to have no culture."

"Excuse me, your highness, but Mackenzie is the best. And she has plenty of culture. The girl plays trombone and is in Spanish II with me. She likes to read. She's a lot deeper than you think."

"Really? I just figured with her liking your pigeon fornication story and how she seems to turn her nose up at Mozart she wouldn't be—"

"Rachel, you're not being very nice right now. Can you please be kind to her? Mackenzie is one of the funniest people I know. Also, she's a musician, so I think she has to like Mozart. And even if you don't like her, don't be rude to her; she's just as new to this school as the rest of us."

Serena quickly walked off with an excuse about field hockey practice starting early. Rachel felt awkward for being scolded and mumbled an "I'm sorry."

Chapter Four

Rachel's guilt complex led to her over-apologizing to Serena the next day.

"Listen, I didn't mean to come across as rude; I just was in a weird headspace and was confused at the thought of pigeon sex and why you brought it up. I'm also just annoyed with math class and Honors English. Will you please stop being mad at me?" she pleaded in front of Serena's locker.

"You were pretty rude at lunch yesterday, Rachel, but that's not why I'm annoyed with you," Serena said calmly while she grabbed books out of her locker.

"What is it?"

"You were really awful to Mackenzie," Serena said. "Are you jealous of our friendship or something?"

"No, I just don't get her."

"Well, maybe you should spend more time with her if you want to understand her better."

"Are you still annoyed with me?"

"Not really," Serena said as she closed her locker and walked away to class.

The next day at lunch, Serena and Mackenzie were talking casually at an empty table when Rachel approached and asked to sit with them.

"How are you guys?" Rachel asked awkwardly as she put her tray on the table.

"I'm okay," Serena said.

"Same," Mackenzie said.

"So, in Honors English today, Miss Wilson gave us example sentences that used pigeons," Rachel said.

"Oh?" Mackenzie asked.

"Yeah, and there were some guys in the class who got lunch detention for writing about pigeon fornication. So yeah..."

"That's hilarious," Mackenzie smirked.

Rachel smiled at her. "Yeah, it made me think of Serena's grandma, although I don't know if she would get assigned lunch detention."

Serena cracked a smile at her friend's sudden openness. Mackenzie furthered the conversation by asking who got detention.

Soon enough, Mackenzie and Rachel realized why Serena thought they'd make great friends and their trio formed. Mackenzie and Rachel got used to seeing each other for lunch every day with Serena and started texting each other outside of school regularly. Conversations went from the mundane of daily life to music to their philosophies and problems.

"My parents can't even remember my own name and sometimes call me by our dead dog's name," Mackenzie found herself blurting one lunch.

"What was his name?" Serena asked.

"Lucky."

"How 'unlucky' for you," Rachel joked. "You think you have it bad? My parents clearly hate me, giving me five billion names."

"Better than getting five billion names because your parents forgot yours," Mackenzie laughed.

The rest of the school year flew by with plenty of lunch laughs, after school hangouts, birthday parties, and silly selfies. On the way to the local bowling alley one day, Serena, Mackenzie, and Rachel were waiting for their friend Michelle Loughlin when they decided to pose like statues and see how long it would take for her to notice. Serena put her hands, balled into fists, on her hips like a superhero, Mackenzie held peace signs, and Rachel gave a demure look with one hand on her hip.

"What the heck are you guys doing?" Michelle laughed as she approached them. She grabbed her phone and snapped a picture of them.

All three of the girls posted the picture online within an hour, and only the three of them liked and commented on it. Serena and Mackenzie added the photo to their lockers. Rachel set it as her phone background. Before the three knew it, they were taking final exams in June and were out of St. Joseph's until August.

Chapter Five

The summer was full of potential plans for the three girls. Mackenzie's family was planning its annual road trip to her Uncle Martin's house, while Rachel's was looking at plane tickets to Verona, Italy for a few weeks. Serena was personally looking forward to sleeping in when her parents suddenly sent her to Michigan to live with her paternal grandparents for the summer.

That left Rachel and Mackenzie by themselves for a few weeks and feeling a bit awkward without their third friend. Rachel decided to break the ice one day and invited Mackenzie to see the new musical movie, *Summer Child*. Mackenzie was happy to get out of the house and thoroughly enjoyed the summer blockbuster. After the film, the two girls got ice cream and talked for hours about their thoughts on the film until their parents found them.

"I mean, Anna Gwin can sing and act, but I would have preferred if they cast someone from Broadway instead, like Sierra Bertram, the original Hester," Rachel said as she held her cup of vanilla bean.

"I get what you mean, but she also killed it at the eleven o'clock number," Mackenzie replied as her cookie dough ice cream started to drip on her hand. "I wish I could hit those notes."

"That's true, she did a good job with that song, but I'll have to show you the Broadway recordings some time, because the original Hester was amazing."

"I'm down for that!"

Rachel and Mackenzie held up on their promise to do something again. They went from movies to minigolf to amusement parks. Both girls' parents knew if their daughter wasn't around, she was likely with the other girl. Rachel and Mackenzie spent every other night at each other's house, having their parents drive them across the city and through traffic to get there. The two were inseparable.

They were on each other's social media stories every time they met in person. All of their approving notifications came from Serena with a comment wishing she was there. They would wish it back before trying to put their phones down.

Mackenzie would play trombone and Rachel would try to follow along on the oboe once she started lessons. They would practice playing music from musicals and then the Top 40 music. Soon, they transitioned from musicals to teen romcoms and would gush over their fictional crushes.

The two even did Honors English II summer homework together while listening to their favorite Broadway actress's, Sierra Bertram, recordings. Mackenzie began borrowing classic novels from Rachel while Rachel learned what it was like to have a big family and loud siblings around Mackenzie's family. Conversely, Mackenzie learned what peace and quiet were while sleeping over at Rachel's house.

They occasionally video chatted with Serena, who kept calling the bottle of soda in her hand pop. It was the best summer ever. One night, after staying up late watching romantic comedies, the girls were giggling and talking about celebrity crushes when the conversation shifted.

"So, what's your type?" Mackenzie asked.

"What do you mean?" Rachel replied.

"The type of guy you like."

"I don't know. I guess I haven't really thought about it much," Rachel said. She paused for a minute, lost in thought. "I think I want a guy who's taller than me but not too tall like a basketball player," Rachel started. "He also has to have blue eyes because those are beautiful and I want children with blue eyes and a good smile. He is probably into a STEM field and also understands that I'm smart and can hold my own in a conversation. He should have short hair and be clean-shaven. He doesn't need a six-pack, but I want a guy who's healthy so I know he can take care of himself. I want him to be at least a year older than me but not like six years older. Oh, and he has to like dogs. I don't know if I can date a guy who doesn't like dogs, or worse, is into cats. I want him to be Catholic too; I don't know if I can date an atheist or anything like that. He should also like classical music and the Broadway stuff we listen to. He will be kind and we'll make out a lot, but he also has to listen to me ramble."

Rachel stopped, feeling satisfied with her answer. Mackenzie stared at her—it was as if Rachel had read aloud the answer to an essay question.

"All I was going to say was maybe he's tall and has a nice butt," Mackenzie laughed. "But he'll also be kind and make me laugh."

"Sounds like we have different types," Rachel said.

"Yeah, those are pretty far apart in terms of specificity," Mackenzie said.

"But what would happen if we met someone who fit both of our types?" Rachel asked.

"I doubt that's possible."

"But what if we did?"

"I don't know, maybe do rock paper scissors over him?"

"I don't think it would be a problem deciding who would date him," Rachel said. "My only problem would be if you knew he was better for me than you and you continued to date him. Like what if I dated someone you were interested in who had more things in common with you and more chemistry with you?"

"Like if Batman dated Lois Lane when she's better with Superman?" Mackenzie asked.

"I don't watch superhero movies. Are Lois Lane and Superman a couple?" Rachel asked. "Is that a love triangle?"

Mackenzie laughed.

"Superman and Lois Lane are a couple. But I think Batman is single for the most part."

"Anyways, it would be the same with you dating someone I liked... or vice versa," Rachel continued.

"That's pretty specific, but I agree," Mackenzie said. "But how would we know if the other person was in love with the guy and they had a better connection?"

"I guess when you know, you know," Rachel answered. "But I think we'll always be friends unless something like that happens. Like, I think we couldn't be friends anymore if one of us dated someone who was better for the other."

"That makes sense, but I don't think that will ever be a problem for us," Mackenzie said. "This all seems too far-fetched."

Rachel switched topics and they continued talking before they both drifted off to sleep.

Chapter Six

Summer moved quickly, and soon Mackenzie was shocked to find she had to transition from sleepovers to getting back in shape for band camp that August. Mackenzie and her bandmates were back to the grind of practicing eight hours a day for five days a week while inevitably getting a sunburn. The football team was running drills, cross country was running in the backwoods, and the marching band was running new music. Being a sophomore now, she had new responsibilities, including making the ninth graders and new kids feel welcome at practice.

On the first day back at band camp, the trombone section was circled out and stretching when section leader, Owen Thomas, made everyone do icebreakers.

"Hi, I'm Owen Thomas. I'm a senior and my trombone is named Jackie," he said before pointing to the girl on his left to start talking.

"Hello, I'm Suzanne, tenth, and mine is Spartacus," Suzanne Fletcher said.

"I'm Tim, ninth, and I haven't, um, named mine yet," Tim Peters muttered.

"It's okay. You can name it whenever you want," Owen said.

"I'll call it 'Cheeseball'?" Tim asked.

"I'm Mackenzie, I'm a sophomore, and mine is named Agent Silver," Mackenzie said.

After a few more introductions, they ended at a dark-haired newcomer on Owen's right.

"I'm Mike, tenth grade, and mine is named 'Veronica'," said the new guy.

Mackenzie was excited seeing the new faces joining the trombone section. She thought Mike was probably the most interesting because he was the quietest and not a freshman. He seemed aloof during practice but followed along step-by-step with the songs.

After practice, Mackenzie tried to introduce herself to him while waiting for her ride home.

"Hi, I'm Mackenzie! Are you new here to St. Joseph's?"

"No, I was here last year and the previous year and the previous year," Mike started as he stared into his phone. "I've been held back for thirty years."

Mackenzie stared at him for a bit before laughing.

"That's funny! But where are you from?"

"I moved here from Philadelphia this summer," Mike murmured.

"Well, welcome to St. Joseph's! It's a cool place," Mackenzie tried.

Mike mumbled thanks before staring at his phone again. Mackenzie would have said more but her ride picked her up.

Mackenzie tried getting closer to Mike to no avail that week. Every time she would try to talk to him, he would blow her off or give her sarcastic answers. She figured he was just sad and missed his friends. She always tried to see the best in people. But when he wasn't playing music, Mike was just staring at his phone, annoyed with the world.

Mike's rude behavior caused the trombone section to run punishment hills around the school, which didn't help with his popularity. After weeks of Mike's behavior, Mackenzie gave up trying to be his friend. And it was just when she let go of trying to befriend Mike that he came back to her.

"Hey, what's your middle name, Mackenzie?" he brought up one day after practice as they waited for their rides.

"Um, it's Joan. What's yours?" she replied, surprised.

"Bartholomew," he said point-blank.

Mackenzie stared at him.

"Really?"

Mike laughed.

"No, but get to know me better and I'll tell you."

"So, are you also really from Philly or was that a lie too?"

"No, I'm really from Philadelphia," Mike said. "I get that St. Joseph's is apparently a cool school, but it's not the same as where I'm from. This community is nice, but the suburbs aren't my place."

"I don't think the suburbs are anyone's place; we all just live here because we have to." Mackenzie smirked and then started nervously playing with her hair.

"Oh, I can fix your hair if you want me to," Mike said.

"What?" Mackenzie asked.

"I used to have long hair, but the principal made me cut it on the first day of band camp," Mike said. "Now I'm stuck with this weird, Beatles, 1960s era hair." He motioned to his sweaty haircut as he grabbed her hair.

"So, what classes do you have this year?" Mackenzie switched subjects.

"I think AP History, Honors Algebra II, Concert Band, maybe Honors English," Mike said. "You?"

"Well, also band and Honors English. Will you have Miss Wilson?"

"Sounds familiar. I think I saw that on my schedule online."

"Cool!" Mackenzie said as Mike finished braiding her hair. She heard the line of cars honking behind her as her phone buzzed. "Well, I should go."

"Hey, before you do, do you want to exchange numbers?"

"Yeah! It'll be good for you to start the year with friends."

The two pulled out their phones quickly before any more cars started honking at stragglers.

✶ ✶ ✶

Michael Jeremy Sienkiewicz grew up the youngest and most sarcastic of his family of five. His parents and sisters, who were older than him by about ten years, doted on him throughout childhood, so he was used to getting his way. When he did not—when he was told 'no'—he would attempt to do what he pleased by any means necessary. This meant his parents weren't surprised when they got phone calls from his school about skipped classes, fights, and getting caught with alcohol at a high school party last year. The last one almost got him expelled, and he couldn't take seeing his parents' guilty eyes by the end of his freshman year. Shame and groundings forever made him decide to change his ways a bit.

Mike's troubled friends gave up on him after he quit his bad habits, so he didn't feel bad when his family decided to move to open a law practice in Brightsville. As friends in Philadelphia distanced themselves from him, he felt himself closing off from everyone who tried to get close. He only missed his friends from middle school who knew him before he made a lot of trouble, and he longed for them as he adjusted to his new setting.

One of the things Mike cared about was playing trombone. He began playing when he was nine, and it was the only thing that kept him focused throughout the day. In addition to his school's music, Mike would spend hours learning how to play classic rock and modern hits on his trombone.

He wasn't excited to start at St. Joseph's and, while happy to join the school's marching band, didn't care that much. When he met

Mackenzie, he felt annoyed. Not by her presence but at starting over again. He figured it was easier to be a jerk to everyone than to let them in and lose them in three years when they all graduated.

But the more they ran over hills and the more his legs hurt as he wheezed, he realized not even his section would like him if he kept it up. He had to let some people in so he wouldn't always be shut out. So, he befriended Mackenzie thinking maybe with her he could survive the first day of high school.

Mike was not attractive. He grew his rarely washed hair past his shoulders and grew out the puberty mustache as long as he could until his parents scolded him. Mike was fourty five pounds overweight at six feet tall exactly. He also had a rash of acne he refused to take care of more out of laziness than anything.

Mike, however, did not care about any of this. He just liked doing what he pleased and never wanted to change when people begged him to. He only cut his long hair when St. Joseph's vice principal threatened to cut it into a bowl cut.

Chapter Seven

As much as school is dreaded, there's always a joy to the first day of school when classmates-turned-best-friends see each other again after being apart for two and a half months. Serena and Rachel squealed as they saw each other and ran for a hug. After a few minutes of fast-paced talking they realized they were ready to find Mackenzie.

The two friends wandered down St. Joseph's halls looking for Mackenzie before comparing their schedules. They had English II Honors, AP U.S. History, and choir together. Unfortunately, they did not have the same lunch on either of their X or Y day block schedules.

"Well, at least we can catch up with each other at the end of the day in choir," Serena said.

"What are you talking about? This sucks. I'll miss you!" Rachel said dramatically. "I'm guessing I don't have many classes with Mackenzie either."

On the school's second floor, Mackenzie walked with Mike to their English class, which they had with Miss Wilson. Mike's hair was just as greasy as ever, now as long as it could be to the student handbook policy before he could be punished.

"Wow, does every classroom have a cross in it?" Mike snarked.

"Well, they used to have posters of nuns angrily pointing, but the school board made them take it away because it made even the teachers feel bad." Mackenzie smiled.

"I wonder what Miss Wilson is like," he said, looking around the classroom. "Is she mean? Hard? Super sensitive?"

Returning sophomores stared at Mike, wondering who the new transfer student was. He ignored the glances and found a seat near the back of the classroom with Mackenzie.

"I hope we don't have to read in this class. That's the worst," Mike quipped.

"Whatever you say, Michael Keith?" she guessed his middle name.

"Wrong."

"Michael David?"

"No."

"Michael George?"

"Do I look like a George?"

"Why not?" Mackenzie said. "I'll figure out the middle name someday."

"You won't. It's a deep mystery."

"Are you sure about that, Michael Anthony?"

Mike rolled his eyes at her.

Before Mackenzie could respond, the bell rang as teacher Renee Wilson ran in late and closed her classroom door. After school prayer and the pledge of allegiance over the speakers, Miss Wilson introduced herself and did a roll call to acquaint herself with her new students.

"Stewart Allen Sanford?"

"Here," a tall blonde boy in the middle raised his hand. "You can call me Stu."

"Okay, I'll make a note... Michael Jeremy Sien...SINESinCUEikz?"

"It's SHIN-kev-itch," Mike announced loudly from the back of the room. "But you can also call me Mike."

"Nice to meet you, Mike, sorry for butchering your last name," Miss Wilson made note of his first while whispering, "SHIN-kev-itch."

Mackenzie gleefully stared at him during the rest of the roll call, waiting for a chance to strike. Mike avoided her gaze, knowing she was going to gloat. After getting their syllabus and being told to prepare themselves to work harder than they did the previous year, most students were itching to get out of class.

As soon as the bell rang, Mackenzie jumped out of her seat while yelling, "Ha, Mike Jeremy!"

"Yeah, I know, you don't need to tell the whole school," Mike said, upset the mystery of his middle name was revealed early due to new teachers.

Mackenzie and Mike walked off to different classes, not meeting until band class at the end of the day. Mackenzie was on an adrenaline high and not just from the start of the day, but also from almost immediately learning her new friend's middle name. Mike was a quirky guy. His middle name was so simple and yet still kind of uncommon. Michael Jeremy? Was that a family name or something his parents just thought sounded nice?

Mackenzie wasn't even paying attention to biology as the next syllabus was passed to her. It took multiple taps on her arm from a classmate behind her to stop daydreaming. Mackenzie didn't want to go through the next few classes. She just wanted to get to lunch, then band, and then home where she could relax and not start her homework until the next day. She didn't have to do her homework until the day before it's due, so she had time.

"Zoning out on the first day?" Ms. Lawson said, looking down at Mackenzie.

"What?" Mackenzie said, realizing she was still in the biology room and only twenty minutes had passed.

"It's okay, Miss Bishop, but hopefully you don't keep doing this every class. Also, if any of you fall asleep in this class, know I'm not afraid to get the class frog, Naveen, out of his tank to kiss you awake."

Chapter Eight

After avoiding frog kisses and surviving the first day, Serena, Mackenzie, and Rachel met at the lockers at the end of the day to go over their findings as new sophomores.

"How was your first day of class?" Rachel asked Mackenzie.

"I mean, I nearly had to kiss Ms. Lawson's frog for zoning out or something."

"Oh, you were fine," Serena laughed. "She was doing that for everyone in the first block today too. I had Kat Howe constantly looking at my notes on my syllabus during that class. Who would already cheat on the easiest day of the year?"

"Oh, trust me, Kat Howe is like that," Rachel replied. "Last year in English I had to do a group project with her, and she made me do all the work. Then we had a classmate evaluation. I saw she wrote on hers that I coasted. I asked Sister Mary Beth to stop partnering her with me after that."

"That sucks," Serena said. "Do you have the one sophomore class with Sister Mary Beth this year?"

"No. Do you?"

"Nope. I guess that means she's teaching the concepts class, so they move at a slower and broader pace."

"Oh."

Mackenzie felt herself getting annoyed for not getting more attention. She wanted to tell her friends about Mike, but she forgot about that as she ran to the band's practice field and caught up with him.

"Hi, Michael Jeremy!" She waived enthusiastically.

"Hush! I need it to be a secret. No one out here has a class with me, so we have to keep it quiet because I need to keep up my reputation."

"Whatever. Why do you want it to be secret anyway and how is a middle name a reputation?"

"Because it's more fun that way. I have a mysterious person's reputation going on. So, if anyone asks, my middle name is Aloysius or Bartholomew, okay?"

"All right, Michael Aloysius."

Mackenzie spent the rest of the practice laughing at the fake names whenever her section had a break. Overall, she had a good first day and came home to her family eating dinner.

"Hey Est— Jun— Mar— Mackenzie!" her mom greeted as she sat down to an empty plate. "How was your first day?"

"It was fine."

"Did you see Serena and Rachel?"

"A little bit. I just have one class this semester with Serena; it was today. But I should have like two or three with Rachel tomorrow."

"That's good to hear... How's band?"

"Good."

"What are you playing again?"

"It's a Queen homage, where we're playing—"

"I'm bored. School was boring today," Junie interrupted as she poked at mash potatoes.

"Maybe it's boring because you didn't pay attention," Mikey yelled at his sister.

Before Mackenzie knew it, her parents were breaking up a fight between her siblings that ended in high-pitched crying and tears. She went off to do light homework before drifting off to sleep.

The next day, Mackenzie was ready to have another easy day. She met Rachel at the auditorium door for Acting I at the school, which was fun with all the improv games they did with Mr. Keenan's instructions. Time flew by, and soon they both were in Bioethics with Sister Tara.

"It's so cool we have classes together," Rachel whispered to Mackenzie, who was in front of her.

"Totally, we can study together," Mackenzie whispered back as she passed the class syllabus to her row.

The two friends laughed their way to lunch. At the cafeteria's entrance, both paused for thirty seconds as Rachel scoped out a free table for them to sit. Mackenzie was looking for Mike but couldn't find him. They settled on some tables near some juniors and ate.

"So next for you is Health?" Rachel asked.

"Yeah, I've got Mr. Bussey. You have Honors Bio?"

"Yep! I hope it's okay. I heard Miss Jackson is hard hearted."

"Well, she's probably good but you heard rumors from the kids who failed."

"I hope. The juniors I've talked to are pretty frank though, so you can never be sure."

"You're smart, Rachel, and you follow the rules, so you'll do good."

"That's what you say. Hopefully, we'll be next to each other in religion in fourth period."

The bell rang and Mackenzie tried to not make a beeline to health class. She couldn't wait to see Mike, who said he had to switch his schedule around and ended up in Mr. Bussey's class with her. He was already in his chair, drawing original characters in his agenda as more and more students filtered in.

"Hey! Why didn't I see you at lunch?" Mackenzie asked as she sat down next to him.

"Eh, I skipped it. Wasn't feeling hungry. How are you?" Mike said without looking up.

"I'm good! I can't believe you also have not taken health class though," Mackenzie said. "This was supposed to be mastered by the end of freshman year."

"I guess I'm not a jack of all trades," Mike shrugged. "But if this is a freshman class, how are you here too?"

"I forgot to sign up for it last year and took Home Economics instead."

"So, it looks like we're on equal footing. But that doesn't mean I won't kick your butt in this class and get better grades."

"Is that a challenge?" Mackenzie teased as the class bell rang.

After getting used to Mr. Bussey's monotone voice for the class, Mackenzie snarked some more with Mike before going to her last class.

✹ ✹ ✹

As the next few weeks went by, Mackenzie got into her rhythm and continued her pace with joy, enjoying her friends and getting to know Mike more.

After texting one night about their neighborhoods, they realized their homes were a half-hour journey apart if they went through the woods. Mackenzie felt a little alone trying the path the first time, but eventually, she and Mike used it to meet up with other classmates in his neighborhood where they would have trombone section bonding at the other's houses. Mike left the inside of his house and his parents a mystery to the rest of the section.

It took a while for her to realize her crush on Mike. She would find herself smiling at the sound of his name. She would tell Serena and Rachel about him often and even mentioned him in conversations about unrelated topics such as Rachel's mushroom allergy and Serena's fear of abandonment.

"Okay, who the hell is this guy?" Rachel interrupted after Mackenzie mentioned Mike's mom's hazelnut allergies. "And why haven't we met him yet?!"

"Well, he's Mike. I'm surprised you guys don't have AP U.S. History with him. He must be in the second class."

"When can we meet him though?" Rachel said. "You keep bringing him up; I want to meet him."

"When are you guys free? We have band practice all week, but maybe I can introduce you to him after the homecoming game Friday."

"That sounds perfect for me." Rachel grinned. "Are you guys going to the dance together?"

"No, I didn't want to ask him because I'm too nervous." Mackenzie blushed.

✸ ✸ ✸

The St. Joseph's Lancers walked away victorious that Friday night after coming back against Central Catholic in the last quarter, winning on a last-minute field goal, 31-28. After the student body flooded the field in celebration, Rachel and Serena eagerly waited outside the band room to meet Mike.

"I'm so happy for Mackenzie. I hope he's great," Serena said excitedly.

"I bet he's attractive; we know all of Mackenzie's tastes." Rachel grinned. "He's probably tall, dark, and handsome."

"He's definitely sweet for sure."

Before they could make more predictions about their friend's crush, Mackenzie hollered at them down the hallway.

"Hey guys, come over here. This is Mike! Mike, meet my best friends Serena and Rachel. You're all super cool people."

They turned around and saw Mike standing next to Mackenzie. His hands were in his pockets as he said "hey" quietly.

"It's nice to meet you. I'm Serena," she said, smiling as she signed her name in American Sign Language. "Do you sign? If so, I'll know not to curse in front of you."

"We've heard so much about you," Rachel said as she calmly tried to shake his hand.

"Same about you both," Mike said. "Want to guess my middle name?"

"What?" Serena asked before blurting out, "DeAngelo."

"Guess my middle name and no," Mike repeated.

"Uh... Jonathan?" Serena guessed again.

"Nope! Rachel?"

"I don't know, Tom?" She shrugged.

"Wrong!"

"Do you know it, Mackenzie?" Rachel asked.

"Yeah, but he's told me not to tell anyone," Mackenzie said. "It could stop the space-time continuum if I utter it out loud."

Mike checked his phone as the girls begged Mackenzie to tell them his middle name.

"Well, it looks like my ride is here, so I'll see you guys," Mike said. "It was nice meeting you, Serena and Rachel."

"Are you going to homecoming tomorrow?" Serena asked.

"Maybe," Mike said and signed "Bye, Serena" before walking away.

Mackenzie turned toward her friends. "So, what'd you think?" she asked after the band room's door closed.

"He was..." Serena paused, "interesting."

"Yeah, he had some nice qualities to him," Rachel said.

"Well, he's a lot better once you get to know him," Mackenzie said defensively. "He's rude to people when he first meets them, but he gets better when you get closer with him. So, I'm sorry if he rubbed off the wrong way."

"But his hair could use a washing," Serena said without thinking.

"I can't help that," Mackenzie said. "I'm attracted to him grease or no grease."

"Well, that's good you see through looks," Serena said. "So long as you like him."

"Yeah," Rachel agreed. "Looks shouldn't matter."

"Thanks, guys!" Mackenzie hugged them both before escorting them out of the room. She knew her friends would support her.

Chapter Nine

The homecoming dance was one of the few times St. Joseph's students got excited about anything school related. Girls in knee-length dresses met up and took billions of photos while guys stared into their phones awkwardly before the doors opened to the school's gym.

Mackenzie, Serena, and Rachel chatted excitedly while handing their dance tickets to the teachers chaperoning the event.

"So, are you going to ask anyone in particular to dance?" Serena nudged Mackenzie.

"I don't know if I can ask him; I'm too scared," Mackenzie said while adjusting her purple satin dress. It was a hand-me-down of Esthers, but it fit perfectly.

"Scared? Why? He's just a guy."

"He could say no and then reject me forever and then our friendship is over."

"He won't! Be brave! Live in the moment!"

"Are you going to ask anyone to dance, Serena?" Rachel asked to end the prodding.

"Well, hopefully Luke didn't bring a date." Serena blushed about the tall junior who was in her art class. "He said he was excited for the homecoming dance on Thursday. What about you, Rachel?"

"Eh, any guy who locks eyes with me during the dance. He'll know it's a sign and dance with me."

"Eyes meet? That's intense," Serena said.

"But it's how you should meet a guy! You don't just approach a guy and ask him to dance. That's improper," Rachel said.

"Improper if you're in the 1890s," Serena snarked.

Mackenzie zoned out from the conversation as they entered the gym, scanning the area for Mike. It became more and more difficult to search for him as more and more students flooded the gym.

The girls themselves got lost in upbeat songs for the first hour and a half before a slow song played. Everyone who was dateless froze in the gym, looking for a partner. Serena made a beeline to Luke Jackson and had her hands on his shoulders and his on her waist five seconds later.

Rachel crossed her arms and rolled her eyes as guys walked by, ignoring her for other girls. She found herself slowly stepping back off the dance floor.

Mackenzie made a lap around the gym but couldn't find Mike. During her search, Owen Thomas approached her and asked her to dance, saving her from potential embarrassment.

After the song finished, most people broke off from their dance partners to go back to jumping up and down to pop music. Serena, Mackenzie, and Rachel ran into each other and started yelling above the music to hold their conversation.

"DID YOU DANCE WITH HIM?!" Serena shouted at Mackenzie, knowing her friends couldn't sign a whole conversation with her.

"NO, I COULDN'T FIND HIM, BUT I FOUND MY SECTION LEADER AND HE WAS NICE! DID YOU?!"

"YEAH! I ASKED LUKE! IT WAS GREAT! HE HELD HIS HANDS CLOSE TO MY WAIST!"

"NO ONE ASKED ME!" Rachel interjected, feeling left out. Mackenzie and Serena looked at her.

"ARE YOU OKAY?!" Serena shouted.

"YEAH, I'M FINE! IT'S JUST A DANCE!" Rachel dismissed.

While they were shouting to hear each other, Mackenzie noticed a large figure out of the corner of her eye moving in her direction. Mike waved to her as he approached the girls.

"HEY! YOU MADE IT!" she said excitedly

"Yeah, it seems lit. I've been here for over an hour," Mike said casually.

"WHAT?"

"I'VE BEEN HERE FOR OVER AN HOUR!" Mike screamed.

"OH, I HAVEN'T SEEN YOU THEN! WE MUST KEEP MISSING EACH OTHER!"

"YEAH, I GUESS! IT'S EASY TO LOSE FRIENDS IN CROWDS!"

Mike joined the girls for the rest of the dance. He got some stares for wearing a bolo tie, an embroidered white shirt, and cowboy boots. He also made up moves and tried to start square dancing with the girls for fun.

"Are you secretly from Texas, or did you steal that off a cowboy mannequin?" Mackenzie asked when the two went to get punch in the vestibule outside the gym.

"I've got perfect style, thank you very much," Mike snarked.

The dance continued smoothly for Mackenzie when suddenly everything turned to slow motion at the last song. As she was about to ask Mike to dance, he casually yelled that his ride was outside, turned, and left. Mackenzie stood there in shock as her two friends were dancing with a JV soccer player and standing against the wall respectively.

Mackenzie would have cried if she was able to process what was happening. She had her moment. She thought they would dance. She was right in front of him, the music playing softly. But he just up and left. Mackenzie stood there like a marble statue.

"Wow, what an asshole," Rachel said as the gym's lights turned back on.

"No, I'm sure he didn't mean it," Mackenzie blurted. "He wouldn't reject me coldly if he meant it."

"I'm sorry, Mack. What happened to you guys?" Serena asked as she approached them.

"He said his ride was here and left," Mackenzie said vacantly.

"It probably wasn't you," Rachel said. "You're a great person, and he'd be lucky to dance with you."

"Yeah."

"It'll be okay, maybe text him later," Serena said. "He seems aloof."

"Maybe," Mackenzie said. "Should I text him tonight?"

"No," Serena said quickly.

The whole ride home, Mackenzie told herself to keep it together. *Keep it together. Be strong. It wasn't you. He doesn't not like you; he's just Mike. He probably was just tired and wanted to go. Guys are weird. Maybe he's never been to a dance.*

She kept texting Serena and Rachel on the drive home, who both replied that it would be fine. It was just a dance, not Cinderella's ball. She didn't need to worry about something so small in the grand scheme of things. It would all work out. They would have to face each other in class Monday, and she could casually mention it then.

Mackenzie unlocked her front door, surprised to see her father still awake and reading in the front room.

"Hey, Mackenzie," he said, looking into his book.

"Hi, Dad."

"How was your dance?"

"It was fine," she said, walking quickly up the stairs. She got to her room, slowly shut her door, and sobbed into her pillow before she could sleep.

Chapter Ten

That Monday, Mackenzie walked into school with her shoulders hunched forward as she wished to disappear from the awkwardness of Saturday. She tried to not make eye contact with Mike as she sat next to him in English.

"Good morning," he said.

Mackenzie nodded with a quiet grunt.

"How's it going?" Mike said.

"I'm fine."

"Are you sure?"

"Yeah."

"Are you mad at me or something?"

"Well, let's just say I'm a bit confused about your sudden exit at the homecoming dance."

"Oh yeah," Mike said. "I didn't realize how awkward I was being until I got home. I should have asked you to dance since you were right there, but my mom texted me at that moment that she was outside and ready to go."

"That was incredibly awkward. Do you not like dances?" Mackenzie asked.

"Eh, they're not quite my thing; I feel a little awkward around crowds. I just go to social gatherings to please people."

"I thought you were having a good time Saturday."

"It was okay. You made it pretty fun."

Mackenzie smiled. "Thanks."

"So, are you still mad at me?"

"Not pissed, maybe just a little annoyed." Mackenzie smiled.

Of course, all of the drama was in her head. Mike was an oblivious teenage boy; he wasn't repulsed by the sight of Mackenzie.

Mackenzie put the dance behind her and continued as she was—daydreaming in class, surviving band with Mike, and finding time to do homework in between. A few weeks later, she was working on an English assignment at home when she got a text from her sister, Esther.

Esther: Hey, bb sis, hru??

Mackenzie: HI! Doing nothing but studying. You?

Esther: So many papers. No motivation

Mackenzie smiled, missing her sister.

Mackenzie: R you seeing anyone at college?

Esther: Does my secret stash of vodka count?

U? her sister added as a second text.

Mackenzie: No, but there is this guy...

Esther: Aww, what's his name?

Mackenzie: Mike. He's in the trombone section with me

Esther: What's he like?

Mackenzie: He's funny and sarcastic and smart. His house is also a half-hour walk from ours if you go through the woods

Esther: Do u guys talk a lot?

Mackenzie: Yeah, we have English, health, and band together

Esther: Nice :) U went to homecoming a few weeks ago, right?

Mackenzie: Yeah, he joined my friends and me during the dance. We had fun

Esther: Did u guys dance together?

Mackenzie: No, but that's okay. There's plenty of more dances

Esther: True. Send a pic?

Mackenzie smiled and scrolled through her phone for a few minutes to find a picture of Mike she liked. She settled on a candid she took sneakily of him during practice a few weeks ago. Mike is wiping sweat off his forehead with his left hand while holding his glasses in his right. Mackenzie sent it to her sister, not expecting her to call her within five seconds.

"Hey, Esther. What's up? Isn't Mike pretty?"

"Mackenzie, are you sure you want to date him?"

"What? Why?"

"He's kinda ugly and he doesn't look like he cares for himself."

"So?"

"Seriously, Mackenzie, if he doesn't take care of his appearance, who's to say he will take care of you? He didn't even try to dance with you."

"He left because his ride was here!"

"Okay. It's just what I'm perceiving here from this pic."

"Oh, it's one picture, Esther. Let me send you more."

Mackenzie sent more pictures, including selfies, group pictures, and posed pictures of him pretending to be a superhero, then waited for her sister's reply.

"This doesn't help. He seems a little out of control and really rude."

"Well, he's a little rude, but only to strangers. And his partying/drinking phase is over."

"He's fifteen and he's had a partying phase?! You're not helping his case, Mack."

"Well so do you at twenty-one, but he's a good guy."

Esther paused. "Is he really a good guy? Has he never given you bad vibes?"

"Well, he was kind of mean when I first met him. He's just a bit rough around the edges, but he's great when you get to know him."

"Mack, that makes him still gross. You need to watch who you're friends with. If he's nice to you but mean to others, that's a bad sign. You're smart, but please use common sense. Please stop hanging out with him. I don't like the look of him."

Both girls were silent for twenty seconds. Mackenzie valued her sister's opinion above everybody else's, but she didn't want to believe what she was hearing. Her sister was really smart and experienced, so she would know these things, but it bothered Mackenzie to go against her feelings.

"Listen, promise me you'll think about it," Esther said.

"I promise," Mackenzie said after taking a deep breath.

She hung up and decided to take a break from homework. Her mother was preparing lunches for the next day in the kitchen.

"Hey, Mom."

"Hey, honey," her mom said without lifting her eyes from her work.

"So, I need some advice."

"You can tell me anything."

"It's about a guy."

Her mom's head perked up as she stared at her. "A guy?"

"It's this guy Serena likes," Mackenzie fibbed. "She has a crush on this guy who is cool and all, but her mom thinks he's a jerk and kinda gross. Her mom thinks he's a douche who won't take care of her, and now Serena is not sure even though this guy hasn't shown any big red flags. And Serena values her mother's input above anyone else."

"Mackenzie Joan, put a dollar in the swear jar first. 'Douche?' Really?"

Mackenzie dug through her own backpack until she found enough change to put in the glass jar next to the decorative cookie jar. Mackenzie's mom then continued.

"I don't know Serena's whole situation with her and this guy and her mom. But think about it like this—what's the fourth commandment? Honor your mother and father. If Mrs. Moore thinks this guy is bad news, Serena should follow what she says. Her mother is wiser in years, and she's only a teenager. You shouldn't worry about it. There's plenty of guys to meet in college. Who's this guy Serena likes?"

"His name is Luke Jackson. He's a junior at our school who is kind of chubby and greasy and rough around the edges, but for some reason, she's really attracted to him."

"He sounds a bit gross and, from what I know of your friend, not her type. But again, her decision."

"Okay, but what if Serena's older sister hates this guy and thinks he's bad?" Mackenzie asked.

"Isn't she an only child?" her mother asked.

"Her older cousin Jess lives with them, she calls her 'sister,' and I guess she also doesn't like this guy and thinks he is a dou—dude who needs to make better life decisions."

"It's Serena's choice, Mackenzie," her mother said. "But if these other family members don't like the guy, Serena should probably take heed and consider their words. They probably know something she doesn't."

"Okay thanks, Mom," Mackenzie said before running upstairs, still unsure of what she was feeling and doing.

Was Mike rather careless? She inspected the first photo she sent her sister and noticed his eyes were wide and pupils were tiny. His skin looked pale, and he had a devious facial expression while looking at his sheet music. Mackenzie suddenly thought it was probably bad to be close to someone reckless. Getting her feelings involved could bring her down. She couldn't think of anything else. She threw her phone on the floor and went headfirst into her pillow, still not sure how to process any of it.

✳ ✳ ✳

The next day, Mackenzie woke up knowing what she had to do. She was going to have to ex out her budding feelings for Mike to keep herself safe, at least for her sister's sake. He had bad vibes, and if staying away emotionally from him meant not having a date by Christmas, then she was a little safer. Her sister was older and wiser and probably was right.

Mackenzie walked into St. Joseph's that morning with a new mission, to ignore any possible situation she could flirt with Mike. He waved to her across the hall, and she gave him a polite royal wave. During lunch that day, she ate in the library to avoid talking to him. All she had to do in the afternoon was avoid making conversations with him in band class. When she got to the band room, Mike saved a seat for her. She froze in place until the class bell rang and Mrs. King made her sit next to Mike.

"Did you see a ghost or something?" Mike whispered to her.

"No."

"You okay?"

"I'm fine."

Mackenzie was a model student that band class, paying complete attention to Mrs. King's instructions and focusing all her energy on the sheet music in front of her. Mackenzie ran out of the class as soon as the bell rang to meet her friends at the lockers. She started packing her books while panting, exhausted from the run.

"You okay there, Mackenzie?" Serena asked.

"Yeah. It's just... I just..." Mackenzie began.

"What happened to you?" Rachel asked.

"I can't be close to Mike ever again."

Rachel and Serena stared at each other and then back at Mackenzie.

"Why?" they both asked.

"I sent my sister pics of Mike yesterday, and she told me to stay away from him because he's probably a bad influence. So now I'm trying to quash my feelings by avoiding all situations where I could flirt with him."

"That's a little extreme," Serena said.

"But I don't want my feelings to blind me! What if I start dating him and then I start drinking or get barefoot and pregnant? My sister is really good at reading people and has great intuition. I need to trust her."

"Would you trust her if she told you to jump off a cliff?" Serena asked.

"That's different," Mackenzie said. "That's something out of reason that intentionally harms people. What she's doing is protecting me, and my mom low-key agreed."

"She also thinks Mike is a bad influence?" Serena asked.

"She thinks I need to listen to authority because they know more."

"That's not the same," Rachel said. "But also, if you don't want to crush on him anymore, why would you still want to be friends?"

"Well, if I'm not dating him like I am already then nothing's going to change right? I won't have him encouraging me to drink or not caring for me if he's at arm's length."

"But—" Rachel started before Serena interrupted.

"Whatever you want to do, Mackenzie, but also you should do what your heart says. Don't be afraid of him just because of one person's opinion."

"Okay," Mackenzie said as she finished packing up.

She ran to band practice thankful she wasn't positioned next to Mike for Friday's show. She needed a break from him but noticed him staring at her during practice. After practice, she yelled goodbye at him from across the field before getting to her carpool's ride. He couldn't know what was going through her head. Mackenzie thought he was no longer boyfriend material and didn't realize her secretly anxiety-ridden sister was projecting on her during a busy week at college.

✷ ✷ ✷

Mike barely understood what Mackenzie's lack of communication meant by the next morning. He kept making some of the same jokes to her which now kind of got a smirk. Mackenzie barely high fived him anymore or made eye contact. Even though they weren't as close now, they were still able to be polite at a minimum and a little silly at maximum. Hilarious was off limits. Mackenzie kept telling herself to be emotionally chaste so she'd stop internally day dreaming about him. Also standing behind him in drills let her see his dandruff.

So, she felt a little sad limiting her time with Mike, but he seemed to respect it. She soon found herself putting more Chris Hemsworth posters in her locker. *Now that's a handsome guy who grooms himself,* she thought. And as the classes went by with the band drills and carpools home, Mackenzie felt better as she interacted with Mike a little bit more and more. Then one day she woke up and forgot she had romantic feelings for him.

Chapter Eleven

Mackenzie woke up that morning kind of excited to see Mike in class. Not to get glances from him, but for his male perspective. Hopefully, he'll listen to her rambles about how her little siblings drove her crazy this weekend.

Mackenzie walked into English class without hesitating to scan the room for him anymore. She knew he was next to her anyway. Mike was reading the newest chapters assigned for *The Great Gatsby*.

"Morning, Mackenzie," he said casually.

"Morning, bro!" she said with excitement.

"Okay, sis!" Mike shot back as he looked up from his book. "Ready for more torture, pal?"

"I like being called 'pal,'" Mackenzie, lightly punched his arm. "Buddy?"

"For the next month call me 'Old Sport,'" Mike joked.

The two stood up as the bell rang and morning prayer began.

After school, Mackenzie found herself talking about her new friendship with Serena and Rachel.

"So now I'm calling him 'Old Sport,'" Mackenzie concluded.

"Whatever floats y'alls boat," Serena said.

"I don't know," Rachel began. "You don't want to date him, but I don't know why you should even still be friends with him."

"What?" Mackenzie said. "Why?"

"Just a variety of reasons," Rachel said.

"Like what?" Mackenzie asked.

"Well, your sister told you to stay away from him in the first place. Not crushing doesn't mean you're not spending time with him. Also, she does have a point that he has a bit of a checkered past."

"Forget Esther," Mackenzie said. "She has dated like two guys in her entire life. I have known Mike long enough to know he's not a bad person."

"That's not the point, Mack," Rachel continued. "Why be friends with a guy you're not even attracted to? He's still kind of rude to people he's met the first time. Do you even sit kind of close to him at trombone event and smell his BO?"

"He does not have BO!" Mackenzie yelled. "What is wrong with you, Rachel? You also come off as rude to people you meet."

"No, I don't; right, Serena?"

Serena pretended she saw someone down the hallway and started yelling back as she walked away.

"Hey I have to get going to field hockey practice, but um, yeah Rachel you are sharp around the edges at first. Got to go, bye!"

Mackenzie hurriedly left for band practice and smiled at Mike when she saw him on the field. Mike made a face back at her as Owen Thomas organized the section. Mackenzie tried to practice undistracted by Rachel's rude comments. Practice continued fine.

Mackenzie was raking her mashed potatoes at dinner when she found herself blurting out to her parents, "Hey, is it possible to be friends with someone you used to like?"

"What happened between Serena and that junior she was seeing?" her mom asked vaguely.

"Oh, nothing. They're good," she lied. "But if Serena stopped crushing on him, could they be just friends?"

"I guess it depends if they started as friends," Julie said. "All good relationships start as friendships. Look at your father and me. I wouldn't have seen him again if our first date was a blind date because I would have thought he was too stuck up."

Mackenzie's father rolled his eyes and laughed a little.

"But he's a great man," Julie continued. "The more I got to know him outside of a romantic context, the more I fell for him. I guess it would be hard to move on after her parents disallowed her to date, but if Serena and that guy wanted to continue talking to each other casually, there's nothing to stop them."

"Exactly, thank you!" Mackenzie exclaimed.

"Did something happen to Serena and her crush?"

"No, but Rachel thinks Serena and Luke can't even be friends."

"That's a little ludicrous," her mom replied. "Maybe she'll come around if you talk to her."

"I hope," Mackenzie sighed.

"How are you, Mackenzie? Are you all right?" her mother asked.

"I'm fine," she said. "Thankfully, the football season is wrapping up soon."

"That will be a good break for you," her mom said. "Hopefully, your grades get better. Are your grades good?"

"Yeah," Mackenzie said, rolling her eyes.

Mackenzie excused herself early from dinner and worked on her English essay about the American Dream tying into *The Great Gatsby*. Mackenzie felt for Jay Gatsby being in love with Daisy, who was pretty unattainable. But unfortunately for the main character, he ended up dead after trying to pursue a relationship with the married woman. So, if he just stayed in his lane or just clearly told Daisy he only wanted to be friends, then no one would've died or been sad, Mackenzie concluded. She would have to be a better Gatsby than he was, minus the money. Maybe if they were friends, Nick would stop judging Daisy so hard.

Mackenzie finished her paper in two hours, resolute on her conclusion. No more Daisy —wait Mike. But hey, even if he was a bad influence boyfriend, maybe he could just be a great friend? No need to worry, right? Mackenzie didn't need a man, but a friend is so much better.

The next English class, she walked up to Mike with her unedited first draft of her Gatsby paper in her hand and stopped in front of him.

"Good morning, Old Sport." She smiled.

Mike looked up from his desk, surprised. "Hey, pal!"

"How are you?"

"I'm alive."

"Alive is better than dead," Mackenzie said.

"Hey, some friends are throwing a party Friday after the last football game. Do you want to go?"

"Of course! That sounds like fun. Who's party?"

"Danny Weathers's. He's in the pit."

"I heard pit parties are crazy. Hopefully, there's no alcohol. My parents would freak if there was."

"If there is, you don't have to drink it," Mike said. "Parties aren't like the ones we see on TV."

"That's good to know," Mackenzie said. "So, then cops won't shut us down?"

Miss Wilson walked by and collected their first drafts. It was then Mackenzie realized part of her essay drifted from talking about owning a nice car and big house to ranting about Gatsby and Daisy's sins because they pursued a relationship instead of staying platonic.

"Crap," Mackenzie muttered.

"Oh, what did you do?" Mike whispered back.

"That may be my worst essay ever," she said.

"It's okay," Mike said. "I wrote mine half an hour before class today, so yours won't be the worst."

Mackenzie smiled before whispering to Mike.

"Can I bring my friends?"

"Rachel and Serena? Yeah, they can come."

✷ ✷ ✷

"Let me prove to you Mike and I should be friends and that he's a good guy," Mackenzie said to her friends after school.

"How?" Rachel replied.

"There's a party on Friday after the game, just come and get to know him."

"A party?" Serena asked. "Won't we get in trouble?"

"They'll have soda for you Serena," Mackenzie replied.

"And how will a party make me think he doesn't have a past?" Rachel crossed her arms.

"Because you need to look at Mike past the grease and what he did last year," Mackenzie replied. "He's a different person now. If you think about it Rachel, the two of you are a lot alike. Hard to meet eye to eye with at first, both of you like music. He's basically an only child since his sisters are out of college."

Rachel paused.

"Ok fine."

"You already know he's a nerd and he likes to dress like a cowboy."

"Yeah true, I need to trust your judgement better. I'll see him better," Rachel admitted. "I'm sorry."

"Whoa, Rachel apologized," Serena said.

"And I accept it," Mackenzie smiled.

✷ ✷ ✷

Before Mackenzie knew it, the week was up and it was the big game. If St. Joseph's won, they would move on to the playoffs next weekend. The game was close, but with a fumble recovery in the last fourty seconds of the game, the Lancers took possession of the ball and forced overtime. The team prevailed in double overtime. The crowd went wild. Along with their bandmates, Mackenzie and Mike hugged each other over the victory.

Mackenzie met Rachel and Serena outside the band room after the game, where they excitedly chatted about the last moments of the game.

"I don't think I can sleep tonight; I'm that hyped," Serena said.

"Nor I," Rachel added.

Mike walked up to the girls.

"Hey, guys."

"Um, we're girls," Rachel said sassily.

"Whatever," Mike dismissed. "Do you two need a ride to the party? Tim Sherman has room in his minivan."

"I don't know if my parents will let me," Serena said, starting to have second thoughts.

"Serena, you can always text your parents that we're having a sleepover and stay with me tonight," Rachel offered.

"Okay, that works."

"Let me just tell my parents we're hanging out with friends before we go home," Rachel said as she looked at her phone.

The girls arrived at Danny Weathers's home with mixed feelings of excitement and confusion. The lights were low, the music was loud, and kids were drinking out of plastic cups. Serena shouted to her friends, "Where are Danny's parents?"

Mike shrugged and went to the drinks table.

"Do you guys want anything?" he asked the three of them.

"Sure!" Rachel and Mackenzie said.

Before any of them knew it, all the girls got separated by more and more partygoers. Serena ended up chatting with some cheerleaders, Rachel found herself with some saxophone players, and Mackenzie was hanging with her fellow trombone players. It took half an hour for Mike to return with two cups in his hands to meet Mackenzie.

"What's this?" she asked.

"Beer. I promise it's grosser than it looks"

"You didn't spit in it, did you?" She laughed. "Also, I thought you quit drinking after your problems at your last school?"

"No to the first question," he said as he took a sip. "I mean, it's one party, right? I'm not drinking to make friends this time at least."

Mackenzie nodded along as she gagged on her first taste of bitter beer. *How on Earth does anyone like this crap?* Her brothers, David, Mario, and John Paul, were self-described beer lovers, but she never really talked to them about alcohol whenever they were home. Mackenzie stared at the drink.

"It's okay if you don't want to drink," Mike said. "Beer's not for everyone."

"It's fine," Mackenzie said. "I don't back down from a challenge."

She grabbed Mike's arm and pulled him into the trombones circle right by them. The trombones played a drinking game before making jokes about other sections playing other games. It felt like five minutes even though it was more than an hour. Rachel was able to make her way through the crowd, drink in her hand, to Mike and Mackenzie.

"I found you!" she shouted triumphantly.

"Yeah!" Mike and Mackenzie said.

"Have you guys seen Serena?" Rachel asked.

"Um, no," Mackenzie said. "Should we look for her?"

"I'm sure she's fine," Mike said. "She's pretty talkative."

"But we should check for her," Mackenzie said. "I know she's a little anxious about tonight."

"No, Mike is right. Serena is extroverted and is probably having fun with whomever she meets," Rachel said.

So, Rachel and Mike started talking about the football game while Mackenzie wondered what she should do. On the one hand, her friend was pretty social. On the other, she seemed nervous at the thought of a party with alcohol. Serena was always worrying about getting in trouble. Mackenzie couldn't make her friend out in the crowd.

"I'm going to go look for Serena," Mackenzie eventually said.

Rachel and Mike nodded as they kept talking.

"So how do you know sign language?" Rachel asked.

"What do you mean?" Mike replied.

"You signed 'Bye, Serena' a few weeks ago," Rachel pointed out.

"Oh, my elementary school taught ASL. I only know the alphabet, hi, bye, please, and thank you."

"I know a little because Serena's father is deaf. Would you like me to teach you some words?"

"Sure!"

As Mackenzie walked away, she noticed how physically close Rachel and Mike seemed while talking. She started reading their body language and noticed Mike making a joke while copying Rachel's hand movements and the latter laughing. They looked animated and like they were having a good conversation. *What am I doing again?* The beer may have finally hit Mackenzie as she stopped searching for her other friend and watched her two companions continue their conversation. She stood there for a few minutes before the pit section leader bumped into her, focusing her back to finding Serena.

She searched through the groups but couldn't find her friend. Eventually, she walked upstairs, hoping her friend was making good Catholic girl decisions. She knocked on some bedroom doors, hoping no one was in there and was about to turn around when she heard a toilet flushing and the sink running. The door opened.

"Mackenzie!" Serena said excitedly as she hugged her. "I'm so tired and kind of anxious. Can we go home?"

"Sure. What makes this scary?"

"I have a bad feeling this party is gonna get busted and I lost you guys. The cheerleaders are also very intimidating people."

"We'll go home soon. We need to get back to Mike and Rachel first."

The girls went downstairs and tried to make it through the crowd to where Mackenzie left Mike and Rachel. Mike and Rachel were not in their previous spot. After looking around a bit, the girls found them talking in the kitchen.

"Oh, I love lemon babka. My family had a maid who would make it when I was a kid," Rachel said excitedly.

"No, my family makes it from scratch; you need to try ours sometime," Mike said.

"Hey!" Mackenzie waved to get their attention.

"Hey, Mackenzie! Serena, we found you!" Rachel said a little too excitedly.

"Can we go home now?" Serena asked, looking exhausted.

"Okay, let's kick this lemonade stand!" Rachel said excitedly. "But who here is sober enough to drive?"

"I didn't drink, but who can give us a ride since I don't have a license?" Serena said.

They all paused for a moment as music and chatter blasted.

"Hang on," Mike said. He looked at his phone and answered it. "Yeah, we're at a party. Can you drive us back and take my friends to their house? We're on 1135 West Blocton Street."

"Who was that?" Rachel asked.

"You'll see," Mike said.

Mackenzie was hoping it wasn't Mike's parents. She didn't want to get in trouble for underage drinking. After five minutes, they walked outside the house and saw a white SUV waiting for them.

"Hey, Mike, what's the password," a woman in her mid-twenties said as she unrolled her window.

"Thank you?" he rolled his eyes.

"Correct," she said. "Now ladies, I hope we can fit all of you in the back there."

"Thanks," the girls all said as Mike opened the back door for them.

As Mike got in the passenger seat, the woman looked at him. Mike noticed her stare and just looked back at her.

"You're not going to introduce me to your friends? How rude!"

"I will! Guys, this is my sister, Victoria. Victoria, these are my friends, Rachel, Mackenzie, and Serena."

"It's nice to meet you," Rachel piped up. "Thanks for driving us."

"Not a problem," Victoria said.

"So, what do you do if you're up this late?" Rachel asked as the car pulled out of the driveway.

"I'm a biologist at the local DNR."

"Cool! I love science too. I think I want to go into STEM in college," Rachel said.

Mackenzie noticed how Rachel was clicking with Mike's sister. It was sweet. She started seeing a connection and wanted to see where it went. After a twenty-minute ride across town to Rachel's house, the girls got out and thanked Victoria again.

"Now don't go drinking for the rest of the night," Mike said to them from the front seat. "I'll then have to call your parents."

"You're one to talk." Rachel laughed. "Have a good weekend."

Rachel turned to the girls outside the car.

"You know what? I actually liked Mike! He was pretty funny once you get to know him. I am wrong again, Mackenzie," she started.

"Yay! I knew you'd think he's a good friend once you talked to him more," Mackenzie smiled.

The girls waved goodbye to Victoria and Mike as the SUV pulled out of the driveway. As they were walking into Rachel's house, trying not to act inebriated, Mackenzie's brain started to click things together. Why was she worried about Mike in the first place?

He was well behaved. And even if they wouldn't date, he seemed to get along well with Rachel. They had a connection tonight. She got along with his sister, which was good. They were pretty cute, actually. Maybe instead of liking Mike as a friend, Rachel should like him as a match.

Chapter Twelve

Mackenzie woke up with a plan the next morning. As Rachel prepared healthy omelets in the kitchen to help her and Mackenzie's light hangovers, the latter grabbed her friend's phone.

"Hey, Rachel, what's your phone's passcode?"

Rachel looked up from the stove.

"Why?"

"I want to add Mike's number to your and Serena's phones in case we ever get separated at a party again and my phone is dead or not ringing."

Serena handed her unlocked phone to her friend sitting at the counter with her.

"Here," she said as she sipped her orange juice.

Rachel paused.

"Yeah, okay," she agreed. "It's 0-1-2-7-5-6."

"That's random," Serena said.

"It's Mozart's birthday," Rachel said as she plated the omelets.

"Ha, nerd," Serena teased.

"I'm not a nerd! You're the one who tries to sign along to music on the radio!"

Mackenzie ignored her friends arguing as she made sure to carefully put Mike's number in Rachel's contacts.

✷ ✷ ✷

Mackenzie stared at Mike during English class that Monday, wondering how to talk to him about Rachel. *Should I be subtle or straight forward about setting them up? How does he even feel about Rachel? They seemed to vibe last weekend at the party.*

"Hey, Mike, how's it going?" she said as she filled out another answer on her worksheet.

"As I told you twenty four minutes ago, good!" he said.

"What was your sister doing here this weekend?" Mackenzie asked.

"She was just visiting my parents," Mike said. "Victoria is a biologist with the DNR two states away and had a late shift but wanted to come home for career advice. That's why she was still up when she got us."

"Does she want to be an attorney like them?"

"No, but she feels like she's spinning her wheels."

"Wow. Well, it was sweet of her to pick us up on Friday," Mackenzie said. "Did you get in trouble with your parents for drinking this weekend?"

"No, Victoria covered for me. You?"

"No, Rachel's parents were asleep when we got home, and then she said we were out at the movies," Mackenzie explained. "So, if they ask, we saw that new two-and-a-half-hour superhero film."

"Okay." Mike smiled. "Can't wait to ask you about Dr. Spacetime in front of your parents whenever I meet them."

"So, what do you think about Rachel?" Mackenzie switched topics.

"Rachel? She seems cool," he said before getting cut off by Miss Wilson asking students to turn in their worksheets.

Well, it was a start to her plan. He had some interest in her, so it seemed. Later that day at the lockers, Mackenzie spoke with Rachel and Serena, asking them about their classes before going in to see if the former had a special interest in Mike.

"Hey, Rachel, you seemed close to Victoria on Friday."

"Yeah, she was really cool!" Rachel said. "It is nice to know women are making advancements in science. I hope we meet Mike's other older sister sometime. Do you know her name?"

"Mary, I think. Yeah, and what do you think of Mike?"

Rachel stared at her.

"I think you already know how I feel. I think he's a cool guy, and I'm glad we're friends with him."

"Okay." Mackenzie smiled as she walked away.

There was a tiny spark, but she needed both of her friends to see what was before their eyes.

The next day at lunch with Serena, Mackenzie couldn't hold it in anymore. It would be more fun playing cupid with a buddy. She swallowed her food while Serena kept talking about how much she hated her math class, then spoke.

"Hey, so what do you think about Mike and Rachel?" Mackenzie started.

"What about them?" Serena said.

"Do you think they would be a cute couple?"

"I'm confused," Serena said. "I thought you used to like him, but now you want him and Rachel together? Am I missing something here?"

"Well, I can't date him," Mackenzie said. "I'm genuinely not into him anymore."

"So why and how does this relate to Rachel?"

"I wouldn't set him up with Rachel if he was that uncaring," Mackenzie started. "But he's not a douche, and I think they have a spark. They're both smart, they seemed to have a really good time together at the party, and she likes his sister. They would fit in together. They've been talking outside of our friend group too. I gave her his number along with yours after that party so they'll be better acquainted. She told me she texted him on Sunday for his lemon babka recipe."

"Okay," Serena said. "So, they might have a spark, but do you know if they like each other?"

"No, but they see each other as friends," Mackenzie said. "Maybe if they hang out together, they'll realize the connection. We should get them to hang out together."

"I guess, but do we know if they like other people?" Serena countered.

"Well, Mike said he was single the other day in health class," Mackenzie began. "But I don't know about Rachel; she doesn't talk about guys a lot."

"That should not be hard to find out," Serena said. "I don't think she'd like someone without telling us."

"It'll work," Mackenzie insisted. "They're really cute together. Think about how they are already happy together as friends. If they were dating, it would increase their happiness and everyone's around them."

"Maybe. I would need to see more of them together to be on board, but I'm not against it," Serena said.

After school that day, the three girls continued their high school gossip. After the small talk died, Serena point-blank asked Rachel if she liked anyone.

"No, why?" Rachel asked.

"Just curious," Serena said.

Rachel switched the conversation to preparing for midterms for yearlong classes and finals for semester long ones. In three weeks, St. Joseph's would be let out for Christmas and New Year's. It was time to gear up for tests, and that was Rachel's focus.

✶ ✶ ✶

One weekend, Mackenzie made sure to invite Serena, Rachel, and Mike out to a downtown Christmas celebration. Stores had sales and garland decorations. There was even a Santa Claus and letter writing to the North Pole for the kids. Rachel and Mike made everyone stop to watch the Christmas carolers perform, during which Serena noticed the two excitedly chat and look at each other when the group performed new songs. It was official, Mike and Rachel were pretty cute to her.

"So, should we do something to set them up now or later?" Serena asked Mackenzie one day at lunch.

"Well, maybe the holidays aren't the right time?" Mackenzie said. "I know Mike's family is going back to New Jersey and Rachel's are going to Vail."

"Okay, we can wait to set them up," Serena said. "I think they could be cute."

"Same." Mackenzie smiled. "Wait until they actually start dating."

✷✷✷

Like snowflakes melting on Virginia concrete, the rest of the semester seemed to disappear. Students prepared for finals with flashcards, had secret Santa class parties, and gave their friends last-minute gifts in front of their lockers.

One day after finals, Rachel, Serena, and Michelle went ice skating while Mackenzie's family left town early for their extended family's Christmas. The girls were happy to see Michelle since she transferred to public school at the start of their second year and wanted to catch up. Any time to see her was a golden time since she was constantly busy with honors and AP classes along with extracurriculars, all while fighting chronic fatigue.

Mike coincidentally was at the rink with some of his band friends and met up with the girls briefly. As everyone struggled with staying on their feet, Serena watched Rachel and Mike skate awkwardly from a distance.

"What are you doing?" Michelle asked as she tried to grab the edge of the rink.

"Watching Mike and Rachel," Serena said. "Mackenzie and I think they would make a really cute couple."

"Really?"

"Yeah, because they are smart and have a cute friendship."

"I guess I could see it if I knew Mike better," Michelle said. "Man, it's hard knowing what you guys are up to after I had to transfer high schools. My parents just couldn't afford it with rising tuition."

"I'm sorry," Serena said. "We miss you. It's been crazy all around this year."

The two then collectively started skating on their own as they watched the potential couple interact. After ten minutes, Mike skated off the rink and left the arena. Rachel skated up to the girls five minutes later saying she was ready to go, so Serena and Michelle followed her off the rink. As they were taking off their skates, Michelle piped up, "So how do you feel about Mike?"

"He's nice! I like him."

"Mackenzie and Serena ship you two," Michelle said eagerly.

"WHAT?!" Rachel asked, shocked. She stared at Serena, annoyed. "Why didn't you tell me? Why would you ship me with Mike?"

"I don't know, Mackenzie brought it up to me a few weeks ago and it makes sense."

"Why would you not tell me about this?! Do you just go shipping people without telling them? That's rude!" Rachel snapped.

"Why are you mad? We haven't done anything," Serena said, confused.

"You've done plenty, gossiping about me and trying to toy with me and my emotions behind my back." Rachel up and left the ice rink to go to her parents' car.

"But we didn't do anything," Serena called out to her friend. She sighed as she rolled her eyes at the thought of Rachel getting together with anyone at this point.

Chapter Thirteen

Rachel fumed to herself for a few days in Vail. It was frustrating knowing her friends were talking about her behind her back, especially about matters of her heart. Rachel didn't like people giving her advice without considering her input or feelings, so getting told she should date Mike felt like getting snapped from a rubber band, especially considering Mackenzie thought for a time he was a potentially horrible boyfriend. Mackenzie knew Rachel's type and Serena probably caught on with Rachel's admitted celebrity crushes, but for them to assume she would be compatible with this guy didn't make much sense to her.

Rachel was even more confused by Mackenzie's nonchalant texts when she first texted her friend in anger after leaving the ice rink that day. Mackenzie was surprisingly calm and supportive. Wasn't this girl formerly crushing and then also semi-wary of Mike? Shouldn't Mackenzie be cautious about her friend dating Mike?

Rachel furiously texted: WHY WOULD YOU 'SHIP' ME WITH MIKE?! DIDN'T YOU CONVINCE YOURSELF TO BE HIS FRIEND A MONTH AGO?

Mackenzie replied: Eh, you have good judgment to see if there are any red flags. You don't believe my sis anyway

Rachel: What about the pact we made this summer?

Rachel started a long text: Wouldn't you be mad that you're better suited for him than me? Wouldn't this get in the way of our friendship? I took what we said that night very seriously.

Rachel saw Mackenzie read the text, but no text bubbles appeared showing she was responding. Rachel kept scrolling through her phone for five minutes when she finally got a reply.

Mackenzie: The pact is fine. Our friendship is strong. But I think he's better for you than me. Y'all are very complimentary 😊

Rachel mulled the text over. *Very complimentary. Yeah, I'm the organized to his chaos. We also have similar tastes and both have moved around before. Maybe we would be a good fit.* So what was her problem with him?

Mike wasn't exactly her type, but he was taller than her, so there was a plus. He was also smart and listened to her science rambles for the last few weeks. He also let her hold her own in arguments. She liked his sister, and if both of his parents were attorneys, then the whole family must be well educated.

Mike's eyes were a pretty shade of blue the more she thought about it. Mike was a bit hard to be around at first, but the more she got to know him, the more she liked him and the kinder he proved to be. The more she thought about him, the more she felt herself growing to the idea of him. He was an exceptional person. There wasn't anything about him that was bad, she thought as she rolled her eyes at Mackenzie's sister's panic attack.

Rachel decided to not think about it as she hit the slopes, went shopping downtown, and relaxed at the spa. Her family went to Christmas Eve Mass and had a hearty supper afterwards. Then, as she started to doze before bed, Rachel's heart raced a little as she got a "Merry Christmas" text from Mike at ten p.m. that night. She thought it was an early Christmas present.

The more she thought that evening, the more Rachel wanted to be with Mike. Her friends were probably right; they would be a good match. Michelle blurting out they should date was a small mistake on her part. Mackenzie and Serena also knew she was aggressive and wouldn't like being told directly to date him.

Rachel waited until midnight to text Mike back "Merry Christmas." It was already a good holiday, but she wished Mike was there so she could see him. She'd see him in a few weeks, but she now wanted to celebrate the holiday with him and get to know him better.

She made sure to text Mackenzie and Serena "Merry Christmas" so they knew she wasn't mad at them anymore. She didn't mean to be rude to them and couldn't wait to share with them her crush epiphany when she got back.

After opening presents and watching movies while it snowed outside, Rachel texted Mike throughout the day. He replied every ten to forty minutes, depending on his family's activities. With every text between them, she became more and more excited as the days passed. On New Year's Eve, after a long day of skiing, she made sure to keep her phone by her side, ready to hear from him at any moment. When the ball dropped, her parents quickly kissed and hugged her, saying, "Happy New Year." With the new year's greetings, she knew with a smile how she wanted her next year to go as she texted Mike back.

Chapter Fourteen

Rachel was resolute on her New Year's resolution to get with Mike. She couldn't wait to tell her friends and make a plan with them to be with him on Valentine's Day. As she was flying home with her family, Rachel daydreamed while staring out the window. She and Mike, holding hands in school, having intellectual debates, her trying his family's lemon babka. It was all so enchanting for her.

While looking down from her plane, she also thought about what her friends were doing at that exact moment. Serena was probably watching TV with her family while Mackenzie was sleeping in until noon. In actuality, Serena was trying to finish the AP U.S. History assignment on time and Mackenzie was out with her favorite sister.

✳ ✳ ✳

In Brightsville's downtown streets, Esther was holding a cup of coffee while Mackenzie enjoyed her hot chocolate. The two were giggling about Esther's latest college rebellion escapades.

"No, I don't think dad would get mad if you told him about the belly button ring," Mackenzie said loudly while passing strangers. "He would get pissed!"

"Mack!" Esther squealed at her before dropping to a hush. "He wouldn't get mad; he would just pull it straight out."

"I can't hear you," Mackenzie said, confused at why she got the piercing in the first place "Is it just there to get guys?"

"Are you sure they didn't spike that drink with espresso?" Esther asked.

"Maybe. You can never be sure." Mackenzie laughed. She was glad she got a morning with just Esther after their family's busy Christmas. As they enjoyed New Year's shopping sales, Mackenzie was excited to buy her own glass Christmas ornaments and a new glass and wooden jewelry box.

Esther and Mackenzie got to a street corner and debated which store to go to next. Esther wanted to try the small home goods store next to them to look at cooking supplies for when she graduated from college and had her own place. Mackenzie wanted to go to the boutique across the street to look at a lavender sweater dress.

"See you in fifteen?" Esther asked as the street's walk light turned green for Mackenzie.

"Yep," chimed Mackenzie as she turned away from her.

Esther turned around and went to the home goods store. Five minutes into shopping, as she smelled scented candles, sirens distracted her from her original mission. Someone was either hurt or a crazy car chase was going on downtown. But the siren's blaring sound seemed to stay outside the store. Esther's curiosity started to peak when she realized her phone's notifications were piling up. The most recent ones from Mackenzie said, "I'm ok. Don't worry. Sorry."

Esther's heart stopped for a second as she found her sister on a gurney. A tall woman in a parked sedan next to the ambulance was standing outside the building looking horrified.

"Are you related to this girl?" a paramedic approached Esther.

"Yes, she's my little sister," Esther replied.

"She was crossing the street when this woman's car ran a red and hit her."

"I'm okay!" Mackenzie croaked, trying to give a thumbs up from the back of the ambulance.

Esther got into the ambulance with her and asked if she called their parents. After five tries of calling their dad, he said he would meet them at the emergency room.

"Hey, Esther?" Mackenzie asked.

"Yeah."

"Do I look pathetic?"

Esther laughed. "No. Only pathetic people think others look pathetic."

"I think I'm still alive from the car hitting my tote bag first. It was full of those ornaments from 12th street and that jewelry box."

Esther opened her sister's bag to find crushed ornaments and splintered wood and glass. Mackenzie was so proud of what her savings afforded her this morning, now destroyed by someone who wasn't paying attention to their surroundings. Mackenzie was released from the hospital that day. She had a bruised left side and bruised bones. Doctors told her family to watch for concussions. She and Esther were happy to be released from the facility after a long day, stunned silent from everything.

Chapter Fifteen

After a few days of rest and relaxation, Mackenzie was back at school the day it opened from break, aching from the pain in her side and feeling fuzzy in the head. She walked up to Serena and Rachel in front of the school's chapel and hugged them as they caught each other up over the last few days.

"I want to say I'm sorry again for lashing out at you guys." Rachel smiled. "You two were right. I realized I want to date Mike. Will you help me find a way to get us together?"

"That's great!" Serena said. "Of course!"

"This is going to be fun," Mackenzie said, feeling unfocused. Her brain felt foggy, like she was at school and wasn't at the same time.

"So what did you guys get for Christmas?" Rachel asked.

"I got some nice hardbacked mystery books and some purple eyeshadow palettes," Serena replied. "What about you?"

"Only this awesome wristwatch." Rachel not so humbly lifted her left wrist to show a dark brown leather band holding a pink and white gold analog watch.

Serena grabbed her wrist.

"It's so shiny! What happened to your other watch?"

"I just keep it on display in my room."

"Hey guys, did I tell you I got hit by a car three days ago?" Mackenzie interjected.

"What?" Serena and Rachel blurted.

"I was crossing the street at 14th and Bull; I had a walk sign when this car came out of nowhere and hit me. I don't quite remember what happened after that. I may have internal bleeding, but I'm okay. Just some bruises on my bones and stuff," she muttered quickly.

"Are you sure you're okay to be at school?" Rachel asked.

"Yeah," Mackenzie muttered before walking off to class. "I'll be fine."

When she got to English, she stood there for a minute scanning for her seat.

"Mackenzie!" Mike hollered and waved from the back of the classroom.

She walked up to him and sat at her desk.

"How's it going?" he asked without waiting for a response. "I got socks for Christmas."

"I got hit by a car three days ago."

Mike stared at her for a few seconds, wondering if she was joking.

"You doing okay?"

She had only told three people outside her family about the accident, but she was already annoyed by the question. Mackenzie was glad she didn't tell anyone over text; there'd be a lot of follow up questions from everyone and explaining what happened over and over.

"No, I'm great! After the hospital, I went to space and met a Martian colony," she rolled her eyes. "I'm their new queen and came to say goodbye forever."

"Okay then. I'll stop."

Miss Wilson turned on the lights in the room to indicate class was starting, blinding everyone but irritating Mackenzie. She was not feeling okay. After the longest day of school ever, Mackenzie was ready to crash on her bed for eternity. Sleep did not help her, however, and the next day she felt even more fatigued.

After three long days at school, she couldn't take it anymore. That night at dinner, she cut her parents' chatter about current events short.

"I am not okay. I'm constantly tired. I can't focus in class. I have this weird fuzzy feeling in my brain. I need help," she pleaded.

"Are you sure you aren't just exhausted from school?" her mom asked. "It's always hard to go back to school after a long break. Or maybe you're just traumatized from your car accident."

"It's been three days, Mom!" Mackenzie yelled. "There's literally nothing to be stressed about! My single-semester classes are now taking it easy, and we just had midterms for the yearlong classes, so we're on new sections! And yes, I am traumatized, but that does not cause this brain fog I feel when I can't even find my seat in English!"

"Mackenzie Joan," her father said. "Don't talk to your mother that way."

"Didn't the doctors say to look out for a concussion?" Mackenzie said. "This is probably it! I think I have a concussion."

"That might be it," her father said. "Are you sure you want to see the doctor? Doctors are really expensive. And we have to be careful about our coverage."

Her father's job's healthcare barely covered anything, and he was happy his family rarely got sick or injured. A concussion would run up her family's bills big time, as if the hospital wasn't expensive enough with good insurance. He was not happy when the ambulance bill arrived in their mailbox.

"Yes!" she yelled.

"Calm down. I'll try to schedule in with a family doctor this week."

"Thanks," Mackenzie said.

"Now apologize for yelling at us. That's not how we treat adults."

"God!" Mackenzie exclaimed. "What is with you guys? I got injured and you act like nothing happened?! I feel horrible, but no, let's worry about Junie not finishing her coloring book or Mikey getting to school on time! I'm sure that will make you feel better at your after-church coffee and donut squad! Because no one cares for their teenager's health anyways! Teenagers who are upset are just acting out and irrational! They'll calm down!"

Mackenzie stood up and stormed off to her room, confused about how she had the energy to get up in the first place before diving into her bead. She locked the door for extra privacy.

The next morning, she snuck out early for her carpool so she wouldn't have to face her parents. She continued the next day like the rest of them that week, dazed and tired.

P.E. class was her release from school that day. Coach Dobbs had the students play volleyball for fun now that the grade books were in for him. Mackenzie was in the back half of the court for her team, questioning the fuzzy feeling, when she felt something flying at her and everything went black.

She opened her eyes to see she was in the nurse's office.

"Honey, you got a concussion," Nurse Lana Palmer sternly lectured her. "You need to see a doctor."

"A what?" Mackenzie asked as she came to.

"A concussion, we're sending you to the hospital," Nurse Palmer continued. "You need to take concussions seriously. If anything else hit you in the head today, you could have died. I'm calling your parents."

After seeing the same doctors again with her parents, they were told Mackenzie was not supposed to be in school. She wasn't supposed to be sleeping so much either since the brain controls sleep. She needed confinement in a room all day for her brain to heal.

The issue was Julie and Jacob Bishop didn't have time to take care of Makenzie. She needed time to recover and would miss St. Joseph's, but she could be homeschooled. Julie had finally started a full-time job, putting her social work degree to use, and was working with the local department of human resources. As a recent hire, she didn't have any personal or vacation time to spend.

After getting back from the hospital, Jacob and Julie whispered to each other in their front room for two hours about what to do. Mikey and Junie were upstairs arguing as Mackenzie was hiding away in her room.

"Well neither of us can take time off," Julie said.

"And we need to save for the college fund and now these hospital bills," Jacob said, mad at his company's insurance.

"What about the family?"

"We don't have anyone close by," Jacob said.

"Yeah, but Marlow and Richard are empty nesters," Julie said, thinking of her sister and brother-in-law in California.

Marlow recently retired as a middle school science teacher, and Richard spent most of his days as the director of the local library. They were free and always offered to watch Julie's kids during the summer. They wanted the kids to go to the beach, visit some theme parks, and take in the weather, which Mackenzie's parents always turned down due to travel costs.

"It would barely cost anything to move her there for a few months," Jacob said. "They could probably help."

"The weather might help her feel better since it's so sunny there," Julie said. So, she picked up the phone and made a call to her sister, knowing it would be a step in the right direction.

Half an hour later, Mackenzie was awoken by her parents.

"Good news, Mackenzie," her father started. "You know how you always wanted to go to California?"

"Yeah," she said, confused.

"We're sending you there for the rest of the semester to stay with your aunt Marlow and uncle Richard. They will be there twenty-four seven to help you and can support you better than we could."

Mackenzie was very confused but that was almost a normal state for her now. After her father stopped explaining and her mother stopped packing her bags, Mackenzie looked at her phone. She stared at it before deciding to open the group chat between her, Rachel, and Serena.

Um hey guys... she started typing.

Chapter Sixteen

Rachel and Serena were quiet for the first time in a long while when they saw each other at school the next day.

"I don't even know what to do," Serena said. "Last week has turned everything around here."

"Nor I," Rachel said. "My parents said to keep inviting Mackenzie to things and texting her to make her feel included so she'll want to come back here after she's healed. Do you think her parents might let her stay there even after she gets better?"

"What do you mean? Mackenzie is their kid and responsibility," Serena questioned.

"Well, her family doesn't have a lot of money, nor do they spend a lot of time with her," Rachel continued. "She'll probably get the attention she deserves out there. Plus, California is better than here. It's not as hot, the people are more relaxed, and there's more culture. She'll have such a good time surfing with beach bums... She'll forget us..." Rachel's words started turning into sobs. A few teachers in the hallway started staring at her, considering whether to intervene in the conversation. Serena hugged her before going off to class.

"It will be okay. I think her parents have to take her back legally. If not, we'll visit her this summer."

Rachel and Serena felt so alone, only having choir together at the end of the day. Rachel felt herself zoning out constantly during the day.

By the second period, everyone at the school knew Mackenzie was out with a concussion for the rest of the semester. Some P.E. teachers took it upon themselves to lecture people about contact sports. Other teachers felt the need to mention looking both ways while crossing the street. The religion teachers found themselves answering questions about the problem of evil. Even the people who didn't know Mackenzie seemed affected by her absence, at least from all the class lectures.

Mackenzie's bandmates approached Serena that day, and Rachel and Mike had hallway conversations about Mackenzie. Everyone seemed to care in a way.

✶ ✶ ✶

A few days later, the girls tried to video chat with Mackenzie after school.

"Hey!" they all said excitedly.

"I can't believe it's you guys; I miss you both so much," Mackenzie gushed.

"We miss you too," Rachel said. "What's California like?"

"Not as hot as I thought it would be," Mackenzie said. "Thankfully, my aunt and uncle are super helpful. They're helping my brain rest, and Aunt Marlow keeps me updated with light school work. How are things there?"

"The whole school misses you," Serena said. "Some randos I met at that party a few months ago approached me today to say they were sorry about you."

"Yeah, and we've already done a rosary in religion class for you, and you were included in the prayers of the faithful at Mass this week," Rachel added. "Teachers and classmates are telling us to send you well wishes and tell you they're praying for you."

"Yeah, some classmates are asking Mr. Anderson why bad things happen to good people, so now we're focusing on that instead of doing busy work in that class before the semester officially ends," Serena said.

"Really?"

"Yeah, and Coach Dobbs has put up posters about contact sports and is now having us play some less harmful sports like kickball," Rachel said. "Never mind the fact that a hit in the head with that would still hurt... Also, Mike said English class isn't as fun without you rolling your eyes with him."

"I've gotten texts from him recently, but he didn't tell me that," Mackenzie said. "Are you still planning on trying to date him?"

"Yeah, if it's okay with you," Rachel said.

"Of course, it is!" Mackenzie said. "I'm just sad I'm missing the beginning of your love story."

Rachel laughed awkwardly.

"No, really, Serena and I had plans to go to dinner with y'all as a foursome, but after getting drinks, we would ditch and leave you two alone," Mackenzie added.

"No way!" Rachel said, trying to look at both of her friends. "That would be so embarrassing."

"It's true, but we can still do something like that," Serena said. "Mackenzie could just conveniently call me and I walk away from the table or something."

"Exactly!" Mackenzie said through the screen.

"So, I guess you're still on board to help," Rachel said. "Please?"

"I'm in another state, but still one hundred percent in." Mackenzie smiled.

"Okay, we've got our work cut out for us then," Rachel said. "Where do we start?"

Chapter Seventeen

When the new semester began two weeks later, Rachel found herself on a high as she had religion class with both Mike and Serena. The school seemed to move on without Mackenzie, but both girls were trying their best to keep in contact with her. They began video chatting with her every Thursday and were constantly on their group chat when they were not studying or doing extracurriculars.

Rachel was ready to start her plan to date Mike. One day after religion, she tapped him on the shoulder and asked him what his weekend plans were.

"I'm going to go see a movie with some of the other trombones," Mike said.

"Sounds fun. What movie?" Rachel asked.

"Bird Brained," Mike said. "The one where bird flu causes everyone's brains to melt and Matt Damon has to save everyone with science."

"That sounds... interesting."

"It's going to be so bad it's amazing," Mike said before getting up. "I'll let you know the scientific inaccuracies after we see it."

He left for his next class before Rachel could ask him to take her. Serena, seeing the interaction, waited at the classroom door so they could talk before heading to separate classes.

"Ugh," Rachel said. "What is wrong with him?"

"I'm sorry, Rachel," Serena said. "Maybe text him and ask him out there?"

"I feel uncomfortable asking someone out over text though," Rachel said. "It's too impersonal and texts can be interpreted in many ways."

"Maybe just keep up with him in general over text, I guess? Instead of asking him out, just carry the conversations you have in-person over from your texts."

"That's not bad," Rachel said. "We can keep the same conversation going constantly."

Rachel took a deep breath as she texted Mike after school.

Rachel: So, do you like apocalypse movies?

Mike: Sometimes. 2012? No. I am Legend? Yes.

Rachel: How many of you guys are going this weekend?

Mike: 10 of us, we're filling a whole van

Rachel: That's cool.

Rachel waited by her phone, anxious for a response, but Mike never responded.

The next day after school, Rachel approached Mike at his locker, ready for answers.

"Hey, Rachel," Mike said.

"Hey, how are you?" Before he could respond, she cut him off. "Why didn't you text me back last night?"

"Sorry, just forgot to respond as I did homework."

"Oh, that makes more sense."

"Yeah, nothing personal, just a lot of math problems to fill out."

"Maybe not this weekend, but would you want to hang out sometime...as friends?" She added the last two words to prevent embarrassment.

"Yeah, that would be fun," he said coolly before walking out.

An exhilarating rush went through Rachel as her hands started shaking. He didn't reject her! He didn't commit, but he also seemed committed to committing to something. Rachel could breathe happy knowing Mike at least saw her as a friend. She could move from there to more than friends. Rachel shared the news with her friends that day over video chat.

"AGH! I'm so happy for you," Mackenzie squealed.

"That's awesome," Serena said. "It's a good start for you guys."

"What day would be good to suggest to Mike? Is Valentine's Day too on the nose?" Rachel asked.

"Yes," Mackenzie said. "You need to be more subtle if you're going for the friends to significant others thing."

"It's just that neither of us has our driver's licenses, so it's not like we can meet anywhere without someone dropping us off." Rachel sighed.

"So, you're probably stuck to school functions for the rest of the year," Mackenzie said.

"There are no art showcases for the next few weeks," Rachel moaned. "How can this get off the ground?"

"We'll think of something," Serena said. "It will work out."

The next day, Serena walked up to Rachel's locker as she was unpacking for the day.

"Hey, what about the varsity basketball game next Friday?" Serena said before saying a good morning. "It's a home game. I can go."

"That's true, but is it awkward going with the three of us?" Rachel asked. "You'd be a third wheel."

"I have that solved." Serena smiled. "I may or may not have already invited Luke to the game."

"Luke Jackson?" Rachel asked. "So, we're already three people without Mike? What if I'm the third wheel then?"

"Well, we haven't bought tickets yet, so you can drop out if Mike doesn't want to go," Serena said. "Mike's more likely to say yes if there's another guy there so he won't feel awkward. Plus, then we could like double date and break off into couples so you can talk to Mike more while I hang out with Luke."

"Do you like Luke?" Rachel asked Serena who was daydreaming about Luke's smile.

"Yeah, was I not being clear?"

Later that day after religion class, Rachel grabbed Mike by the shoulder.

"Hey, Mike, want to join Serena and me at the basketball game next Friday? Serena is bringing this junior, Luke Jackson, so I don't want to be the third wheel in case she has other intentions."

"Yeah, I can go," Mike said. "What time is the game?"

"Seven thirty. It's a home game as you know."

"Is that p.m. or a.m.? I don't want to wake up extra early and miss class for this game," Mike joked.

Rachel laughed. "You know what time it is, imbecile!"

"Do I? I'll see you there then," Mike said.

Chapter Eighteen

Serena got to the basketball game half an hour early the next Friday, anxious to be there before tip-off. She thought Luke was attractive and funny and wanted to go to his prom with him this year since she was still an underclassman.

Serena was surprised he said yes to the game because they didn't have a class together since the end of the last semester. But he always said hi to her in the hallway and they were following each other's social media accounts. As she waited at the tickets table, unsure whether to buy a ticket for herself or two for the both of them, Rachel walked up to her.

"Hey, you're early," Rachel said with a nervous laugh.

"As are you," Serena replied.

"I can't believe it's happening," Rachel said, checking her phone to find encouraging texts from Mackenzie. "I'm scared but elated at the same time."

"Don't worry, I'm also nervous," Serena said, staring at her phone, not paying attention to her own words.

A few minutes later, Luke showed up and walked over to the girls. He paid for everyone's tickets, including Mike's, who wasn't there yet. The group stood outside the gym waiting for Mike before looking for seats.

It was twenty minutes until tip-off, then fifteen, and then ten, and Mike was still absent. Rachel kept getting nervous the more he didn't reply to her texts.

"Hey Luke, want to get some seats while Rachel waits for Mike? Not all of us need to be out here," Serena said.

"Sure, if Rachel's fine with that," Luke replied.

"I can wait." Rachel nodded. "You guys go get good seats."

Serena and Luke headed into the gym. Rachel waited until she heard the national anthem to find her seat next to Serena and Luke.

"He's still missing?" Serena asked.

"Well, he's not here," Rachel replied.

"I'm, um, sorry… Rachel," Luke interjected awkwardly. "He's probably just late for a good reason."

Five minutes after the tip-off, the group was alerted to Mike's presence after hearing him apologize for bumping into people as he walked through the stands.

"Hi...hey...hello," he said to all three of them individually. He turned to Rachel. "Sorry I was late; traffic was a nightmare."

"It's okay!" Rachel said. "I think these are our basketball team's rivals."

Mike nodded before paying attention to the game. St. Joseph's was losing to the St. Bridget's Dragons by five points, and while Rachel tried to make small talk with him, she realized he was actually watching the game. Rachel soon found herself interested in the basketball game too.

Mike would only engage with Rachel when she tried starting conversations during slow moments of the game. He also tried starting the wave across the stands, but only he, Rachel, Serena, and

Luke would do it. Serena turned to Luke and began chatting with him to give Rachel and Mike privacy.

"So, how's your semester going so far?" Serena asked.

"Not as fun without art," Luke said. "Classes are more intense."

"Yeah, same. AP U.S. History is ramping up for exams even though it's not even February."

"APs are such a pain," Luke said. "Dunleavy is going to give you a slew of projects this semester."

"Oh crap." She facepalmed. "Thanks for the warning."

Serena and Luke kept talking when they were interrupted by Mike and Rachel laughing.

"What's up?" Serena asked them.

"Oh nothing." Rachel continued to laugh. "Mike made a pun in French. You and Luke take Spanish, right?"

Serena and Luke shrugged.

The basketball game was quick-paced but felt slow to Rachel, who was constantly trying to capture Mike's attention whenever he turned from her. But like the first half of the game, not even she could pay attention to the person beside her as the Lancers kept making three-point attempts. St. Joseph's lost at the last second when a tall point guard from the other team made a buzzer-beater.

"That was a crazy game," Serena said as the group left the gym.

"I know!" Rachel replied. "I thought we had it!"

The girls chatted excitedly as Luke and Mike walked quietly behind them. Mike checked his phone and responded to a text.

"Well, this was a fun night, but my ride is here," he said. "See ya Monday!"

"Bye, Mike," Serena said.

"Bye, Sienkiewicz," Luke said.

"Goodbye, Mike. Have fun this weekend," Rachel called out to him.

✷ ✷ ✷

"Are we sure Mike isn't gay?" Serena asked Rachel and Mackenzie over video chat that night. "He didn't show much interest again. I don't know."

"No!" Mackenzie insisted. "I know his celebrity crush is Taylor Swift. He's told me about his former crushes from New Jersey."

"And those ladies couldn't have made him realize he's gay?" Serena suggested.

Rachel rolled her eyes. "If you ship us, then you should think he isn't gay. He would be at least bi."

"That's true, but what if we're wrong?" Serena asked. "Then aren't we harassing him?"

"Serena, I can assure you he's not gay or bi," Mackenzie said before hesitating. "Don't tell anyone this, but at a bones and sax hangout last fall, we played truth or dare and someone else asked if he was gay. He said no. He was also dared to kiss the hottest person in the room and kissed sax member Jessica Klein."

"Wow," Serena said. "Did that sting, Mack?"

"I was getting over him enough when it happened."

"Jessica looks okay enough. I don't know what she saw in her," Rachel mumbled. "She seems to like makeup more than grades."

"Point is, he said he's watched bad films just because they had Taylor Swift or some other woman in them. You do that with male celebrities, Serena," Mackenzie said defensively.

"I do love Ryan Reynolds." Serena paused. "Even so, it was awkward how uninterested he was with anyone at the game. He mainly watched the game and left without making any further plans."

"Maybe he was busy?" Rachel asked. "He is also an AP and honors student."

"Yeah, but he also arrived late. Even if traffic was bad, he still left the house late when he could have planned ahead of time," Serena pointed out.

"Yeah, well, Luke wasn't paying attention to you either the whole game," Rachel said defensively.

"We were watching the game," Serena replied.

"I think Mike just saw it as a group hangout because you asked him out as friends," Mackenzie said. "But maybe it went well enough tonight that he'll want to continue hanging out together. And while you continue to do so, he'll realize how great you are and want to date you."

"That's true," Rachel said. "Maybe he'll participate in the school's carnation sale and we'll end up exchanging flowers."

"Yeah!" Mackenzie said excitedly before hanging up to eat dinner with her aunt and uncle.

Rachel hung up, frustrated with her friends but glad she got one step closer with Mike.

Chapter Nineteen

A few weeks later, St. Joseph's held its annual carnation fundraiser where students gave and received carnations on Valentine's Day. Give money, write on a card to whoever you wanted to talk to, and hand it back to those working the table. One for a dollar and fifty cents, five for five dollars, and all the proceeds went to the religion department.

Various students from all grades crowded the fundraiser table at the cafeteria. Rachel was intimidated buying carnations for the first time but figured she could play it off if Mike asked. She would buy some for Serena and a few other friends because she had five dollars on her. She shuddered from nerves as she walked up to the table.

"Hi, can I buy five?" Rachel asked.

"Sure!" said one of the freshman girls sitting there. "You must have a lot of good friends."

"You could say that."

Rachel filled out a card for Serena first: "Thank you for being an awesome friend!"

She paused to think of who else she could send some to. She sent one to Mary Kate Love since she attended the opera with her last year: "Happy Valentine's Day"

Fellow soprano ones' Larissa Bell and Amy Smith are also hardworking, so why not? Rachel thought as she wrote their names down: "Good job hitting above C at the concert."

Last was Mike's. Rachel stared at the blank, small notecard. Should she show emotion? How much is too much to write? Should she even try to flirt? Maybe just write "Happy Valentine's." No, she had to go for something else.

Rachel awkwardly grimaced as she wrote down: "Mike, you are a really fun person and I like getting to know you as a friend better and better every day. Happy St. Valentine's Day! With Care, Rachel Hoyt." With that, she handed the card and the pen back quickly to the girls at the table.

✱ ✱ ✱

Rachel was pleasantly surprised when she found three carnations at her homeroom desk on Valentine's Day. She looked through the cards carefully. There was one from her Honors Algebra II class leader and one from Serena. Her heart started racing when she saw the third had a tag from Mike.

She turned over the note from Mike, hoping for some encouraging words, but was disappointed to see it blank. That was a little weird. What did he want to say? Why think of someone enough to get a carnation for them and have it be empty? If he didn't like her, why would he send a flower in the first place? At least now Rachel knew she was somewhere on his emotional radar and that gave her some hope.

While she scanned the busy cafeteria at lunch, she heard Mike calling her name. He was at a table with friends and waved her down.

"Hey! Why are you here?" Rachel asked excitedly.

"Dunleavy let us go early," Mike said. "Thanks for the flower. Want to sit with us?"

"You as well!" Rachel smiled as she sat down. She was in with his crowd, and she was going to take her sweet time to talk to him and befriend his friends.

Mike introduced Rachel to everyone at the table, and they talked about their homework and how many flowers they got. Mike told them all Rachel was the only person who sent him one.

"I'm sorry," Rachel said concernedly.

"Don't be," Mike said. "I don't really care about flowers, but it's a nice gesture."

"Well, duh," Brian Sosa said from across the table. "Everyone wants to be cared for, dude. You shouldn't keep all of your emotions bottled up."

"Yeah," Rachel said. "I'm just glad I got three. Did you send any to any other people?"

"Yeah, one to Brian here, who didn't reciprocate, and to all the other trombones."

"Well, I don't know if those trombones can use them since they are lifeless," Rachel said, trying to make a quip.

Mike paused for a second, trying to get what she was saying.

"Good one. I did and now those poor flowers will die unappreciated."

Rachel laughed along with the table. It was so good to talk with Mike. She was feeling a connection growing, but she was also a little disappointed she wasn't the only girl he sent a flower to that day. Trying to look pleased, she decided to change the topic.

"Okay, Mike, candy hearts or chocolate for today?" Rachel asked.

"Candy hearts," Brian voiced his opinion.

"Thanks for answering, Mike," Mike retorted. "But I guess I am right. Chocolate is sometimes too much for my tastebuds."

"Oh okay," Rachel said, axing the idea of inviting him to buy discounted chocolate tomorrow.

"What about you?" Mike asked.

"I like chocolate better," she said. "Candy hearts are chalky."

The lunch bell rang and everyone got up for class. Rachel was proud of the progress she made with Mike on Valentine's Day. She wasn't where she wanted to be in progress to getting with Mike, but she was still on track. He gave her a flower! Of all the people he chose, she was one he thought of who also wasn't in marching band with him, so she held her head high as she walked to Honors Algebra II. She was extra grateful that Mr. Dunleavy decided to let his students take an earlier lunch for whatever reason. She thanked class leader Lucy Lassiter as she went to her seat and couldn't focus for the rest of the day. By the last class bell, she was quietly celebrating her victory with Serena.

"That's amazing!" Serena said. "What color flower did you get from him?"

"Just pink," Rachel said, pulling it out from her carnation trio. "How many did you get?"

"Four," Serena said. "Yours—thanks, by the way—some from my field hockey teammates, and the white one is from Luke."

"Nice!" Rachel said. "Have you spoken with him today?"

"Yeah, we passed each other in the hall and thanked each other."

"I can't wait to tell Mackenzie about this," Rachel said, looking at her carnations. "Do you think she'll be surprised?"

"Totally, she's going to squeal in excitement."

"Good," Rachel said. "I'm going to go say goodbye to Mike and see if he wants to hang out this weekend."

"Good luck!"

As Rachel went down the halls to find Mike, she saw his locker was deserted. She asked classmates if he was near, and they pointed her to Mr. Anderson's classroom. She found Mike walking out of mercy detention fifteen minutes after school ended.

"Mike? Mercy detention? What did you do?" Rachel asked.

"I killed a priest," Mike snarked.

"Better than killing a nun."

"Or Mr. Anderson."

"So, hey, what are you doing this weekend?"

"The trombones are doing their service retreat out of town this weekend. Did you want to hang out?"

"Sure! That would be fun!"

"No, I meant were you hoping to hang out?"

Rachel felt awkward. "Well, yeah, but it's fine that you can't," she mumbled.

"Okay. We'll do it another time," Mike said as he walked outside the school.

Rachel went home with mixed feelings. She was going one step forward and two steps back with Mike. She thought she was trying to speed things up too fast with him, but he was also taking things very slowly. Maybe she would have to join an activity with him to get him to notice her. She kept those thoughts to herself until she could contact Mackenzie later that evening.

Chapter Twenty

Rachel decided to distract herself from Mike by signing up for the orchestra pit for the school's upcoming production of *Singin' in the Rain*. Her year of practicing oboe was going to good use. There weren't auditions for the pit, so she walked into the band room the first day of practice and was surprised when she heard Mike call her name as he sat in his chair.

"Hey, Mike! You're doing pit?" Rachel asked, surprised.

"Yeah, it seems like fun," Mike said. "My sisters like this musical, and I figured it was something to do for them. I didn't know you were a musician. What instrument do you play, Rachel?"

"Oboe," Rachel said. "I've been practicing for a year just to have another activity to do. I don't play with others often because of how busy this school keeps us."

"Well, I just hope these theatre kids can sing. It would be a shame to waste perfectly good music on them," Mike replied.

"Mr. Keenan and Sister Mary Beth are usually particular with casting, according to some of my choir classmates. Whoever they cast for the female lead will be excellent since there are probably more girls auditioning. For guys, it might be slim pickings."

"Do you think they're going to have to pull in guys from Sister Mary Beth's class?" Mike asked. "I've heard that she's done that before."

"Hopefully not," Rachel said. "They've only done that once and it was because they didn't have enough students for Frankenstein."

"Frankenstein didn't have enough people to approach him with torches and pitchforks?" Mike snarked.

"Well, technically Dr. Frankenstein's monster, but also for just terrified villagers in the first place."

Rachel wasn't worried as she and Mike left the pit's first meeting. She didn't have to ask him out now; she had plenty of time to be with him and could get to know him better during the musical. For once in her life, Rachel's plans with Mike seemed to go right. Every day after school, she would meet Mike outside the band room and chat with him, make eye contact during rehearsal, and then talk with him until her ride home arrived.

The one thing bothering her was waiting to get her driver's license so she could take herself to and from wherever she chose at any time. Her birthday wasn't until June, so she would have to keep being patient and work with her parents' schedules.

What she didn't realize three weeks into rehearsals was that Mike recently turned sixteen. One day in religion class, he casually told her he was about to get his license after school and miss practice.

"You're old enough to drive?" Rachel asked, shocked. "Did you turn sixteen recently?"

"Yep."

"Why didn't you tell me?"

"I don't like having to tell people my birthday over and over again. I'd rather they just remember it without social media notifying them."

"But how will we know if it's your birthday if you don't tell us?" Rachel asked.

"Well, you can ask me anytime," Mike said. "When's your birthday?"

Rachel paused for a moment. It never occurred to her to be that straightforward and ask someone for their birthday. It was something she had done when she was a child in elementary school but stopped when she aged.

"Um, June 22," Rachel said. "I'm sorry I missed your birthday and that I never asked about it in the first place."

"It's really not a big deal," Mike said. "I don't really care for birthdays."

"You're only sixteen."

"Okay, but like to people in the Middle Ages, I'm super old."

After class ended and students were packing, Mike leaned into Rachel to ask, "Hey, when I get my license, do you want me to just drive you home from musical rehearsal?"

"That would be great!" Rachel felt her awkwardness melt away.

She tried to be casual that night at dinner when her parents asked her about her day.

"Who inspired you today?" Rachel's mother asked while cutting her chicken piccata.

"Um, well the pit did a good job on 'Singin' in the Rain' and 'Moses', so I would say everyone since we did well as a team," she replied.

"That's wonderful, Rachel!" her father went. "Did you learn any new words today?"

"Dad, I'm fifteen, not five," Rachel snapped. "I don't even have Honors English today."

Rachel was used to her parents using alternative questions to "how was your day" and she usually played along, but the baby questions irked her.

"Okay, instead of a word, how about what made you smile today?" her father asked.

Rachel hesitated. The high of her day was Mike offering to drive her home from practice, but she didn't want to get bombarded with questions. But she wanted permission to go home with him instead of waiting for her parents, and the reward was worth the risk.

"A friend of mine and Mackenzie's is getting his driver's license, and he's offered to drive me home from rehearsals, if that's okay," she said. "He's also in the orchestra pit. It would mean I wouldn't have to wait half an hour for you guys to pick me up; I could get a start on homework sooner."

"That would be convenient for us," Rachel's mother said. "What's his name?"

"Mike Sienkiewicz, and he is also in the marching band with Mackenzie."

"We'll have to meet him someday." Her father smiled. "We're glad he'll help, and we'll pay for his gas if he's willing."

Rachel was surprised at how easy it was to get her parents on board. But any mention of Mackenzie usually brought goodwill to them, so that helped.

Thanks, Mackenzie, she thought as she loaded her fork full of capers. Tonight's video chat would finally bring good news.

Chapter Twenty-One

Riding in Mike's car was anticlimactic for Rachel. She braced herself every time they left the school. Mike's car was a minivan from the early 2000s whose lights came on whenever he drove over a speedbump. The car was generally messy from him eating breakfast on the way to school and his windows did not fully roll down.

"I call it Shirleen," Mike told Rachel the first time she saw it after their pit rehearsal. "Because it's pretty old and cooky like your average senile grandma."

"I don't think that's an actual name," Rachel said.

"Sure, it is," Mike said. "It's my car's name."

As bad as Shirleen was, Rachel enjoyed the time spent with Mike. He listened to the same kind of music as she. The two also always had something to talk about whenever they went home, whether it was practice, school, or music. The one thing Rachel couldn't get Mike to do was open up about his life or suggest they do something together.

Up until the school's musical debut, the car rides continued the way they were, without any success for Rachel.

Other than when an actress forgot a line and an actor pulled from Sister Mary Beth's class entered late, the Friday show went perfectly. The audience didn't notice; they hadn't studied the show. Rachel and Mike gave sighs of relief after their debut. Rachel's parents attended Saturday's show and approached Mike as the students packed their instruments in the band room.

"You must be Mike," her father said with a hand stretched out toward him.

Mike shook it and said, "Sir."

"You guys played great tonight," her father added. "We could hear you well enough without your music overpowering the actors. It was perfect."

"Thanks, sir," Mike said.

"We also appreciate you safely driving our only daughter Rachel home from rehearsals the last few weeks," her mother said. "We're happy Rachel has another person at this school she can call a friend."

Rachel blushed from all of her parents' comments, hoping they would leave soon. Granted, that meant less time with Mike, but she'd take less of him over more of her parents talking to him.

"Well, thanks for coming out," Rachel said, quickly escorting her family out of the school to the car. "I'll see you tomorrow, Mike."

Sunday's matinee show went well enough until Rachel hit a wrong note by mistake during a song and a few audience members laughed. Rachel felt herself crumble from the feedback after the show, shaking as she packed her instrument. Mike and Serena tried to be her cheerleaders.

"It's okay," Mike told her afterward. "The show is over forever anyway, and it didn't ruin the show."

"You did great, Rachel!" Serena piped up. "I didn't notice anything until some stupid jocks started laughing, but they could have been making a joke about something else instead of the note. Kate Parsons made some awkward faces during the show, that may have been it."

"Yeah, that was probably it," Mike said.

"I guess," Rachel said.

"You worked really hard, Rachel," Mike said. "It was great playing with you. Even if you made a mistake, it's what performers do. You'll get new sheet music and move on to the next performance."

Rachel couldn't help but smile a little after Mike's pep talk. She spent most of her time at the cast and crew wrap party by Mike's side. She dreaded the party ending and not getting to ride home with him again after tonight. After all the cake was eaten and students grumbled about getting homework done, she and Mike went to his car.

The drive was a little quiet between the two of them. To fill up the silence, Rachel started talking about her favorite spring activities, including biking and bird watching. Mike laughed at her.

"Do activities just come seasonally to you? Like you don't ride your bike in any other season?"

"No, but it's something I associate with the nice weather."

As Mike pulled up to her house, he said, "I have to confess something."

Don't panic, don't panic, don't panic, she thought as her heart raced, thinking he was going to say he knew she liked him but he didn't feel the same.

"I've never…" Mike started.

BADum. BADum. Rachel's heart pounded.

"…ridden a bike before," he finished sheepishly.

Rachel stared at him for thirty seconds, trying to comprehend what just happened.

"I'm sorry, what?" Rachel said.

"Well, my most of my family live in the city, so I never got around to it."

"You can ride bikes in the city! What about your friends? Didn't they ever invite you to ride bikes or an extended family member give you one for a birthday?"

"No, why would they do that?"

"Because it's fun," Rachel said while getting out of the car. "I think I have a new mission in life—teach you to ride a bicycle."

Mike laughed as he drove away, not realizing Rachel was being serious. She stood on her porch as his car backed out, already thinking of the different kinds of bikes she could get him and where to teach him.

Rachel daydreamed that night about the upcoming summer. Mackenzie would be back so they could hang out. Mike and Serena would be there too so she expected good times. She would get a summer job and teach Mike how to ride a bicycle in her free time. She could see him trying and falling over a few times but then getting up and laughing. They would have fun racing their bikes in the park, and by the time they reached the local coffee shop, he would ask her out. With their new drivers licenses and parents' cars, he would take her somewhere romantic, like downtown or the park.

These daydreams comforted Rachel as she went through AP exams, final class projects, and tests with the rest of the St. Joseph's student body. Rachel and Serena were now counting down the two weeks before Mackenzie returned. During that time, Serena got a job scooping ice cream for minimum wage and Rachel planned on working as an assistant at her parents' office.

Serena was determined to talk to Luke before school ended and they were separated for ten weeks. Rachel high-fived her as she walked up to her crush, standing alone by his now empty locker. Rachel couldn't hear them from one hundred feet away, but since the conversation was reaching five minutes, she figured someone was talking about their feelings.

Oh no, Rachel thought as she saw Serena begin to shake. Luke hugged her. They pulled apart as he hugged her again. The two went separate ways down the hall as Serena's mascara tears became darker and darker. Rachel hugged her as they walked out of the school.

"I don't get it," she sobbed to Mackenzie and Rachel over video chat that evening. "We spent all that time together. I thought he was into me. He paid attention to me and always checked up on me. He would also send me a lot of winky faces in texts. How could he not like me and ask out another girl?"

"It's okay. Maybe he just doesn't realize it yet," Mackenzie said. "Maybe he'll date this girl and hate her and realize how great you are like in all the romcoms."

"Maybe you should have picked up on the signs he doesn't like you," Rachel said abruptly.

"Rachel!" Mackenzie chided her.

"Sometimes guys just don't like you no matter how great you are, and it sucks. But you can't keep pursuing someone who won't give you the time of day," Rachel said. "If he really likes you, then he'll come around. Sometimes there are no good answers, as frustrating as it is, to why a guy doesn't like you. But Serena, you're stronger than this, and you will find a guy who is into you who you'll like back."

For Rachel, it was still going to be a good summer, until Mike said he was going to New Jersey for the summer to reconnect with friends. Her hopes were still high when he told they could video chat.

Mike: It's going to be a good summer. You're not going to miss me

Rachel: I promise I won't. :p

Mike: Good

 Mike put down his phone for the rest of the evening as Rachel stared at hers, wondering what to type next.

Chapter Twenty-Two

"Your concussion is gone and you're all clear to go back to school, Miss Bishop," Dr. Bradley Calvin told her at his office the last week of May.

"Yes!" Mackenzie cheered as she fist-pumped the air.

Mackenzie's parents both gave sighs of relief and thanked Dr. Calvin after he gave them all the good news.

"Well, Mackenzie, it seems you're good on the health end," Dr. Calvin said. "Do you play any contact sports?"

"Soccer and I'm in marching band," she said.

"No soccer for six months, okay? We want to keep that head of yours good and safe," he said.

"Okay." She wasn't worried about soccer since she missed last season anyway and sat on the bench all of freshman year. Mackenzie figured it was time to move on from the lost cause.

After her doctor's appointment, Mackenzie's parents drove her to St. Joseph's to talk to the vice principal about readmission. So far, class reenrollment was going well. The school didn't have competitive spots for her to give up a seat.

"We just need you to sign some papers to re-enroll for next year. Your financial aid should carry over from last year," Vice Principal Shawn McNelson said. "However, we will need to test you before you start school to make sure you're academically ready for junior year."

Mackenzie internally panicked at this part of the meeting. She had the course credits. Her Aunt Marlow kept her on her toes in the spring semester with learning, sometimes making her learn answers to a song and dance, other times by talking to the math problems. She felt like she could handle it, but what if the exams weren't enough? She'd be one grade behind but hundreds of emotional miles away from her classmates as well.

Mackenzie spent two weeks studying for her junior year preparedness test during June. Her tests were a week after St. Joseph's let out, and her parents didn't want her friends to bombard her when she just got home. So as Rachel and Serena counted down the days to see her, she counted down the days until she had to take her do-or-die exams. The day of the exam, Mackenzie was lightly hyperventilating before the test.

"It's just a test; you'll do great," Miss Wilson said. "You know this material, and judging from your grades in my English class, that concussion did not knock the answers out of your brain. Just focus and you'll do well."

Just focus. That's right, just regulate your breathing and you can do it. Mackenzie kept repeating this to herself as she sat in a cold desk in an empty classroom. She kept breathing slowly, taking in the smell of floor cleaner maintenance was finally able to apply without the buzzing student population all over the place. Mackenzie had to tell herself to focus as Miss Wilson proctored the test.

What's my name? Mackenzie thought as she looked at the scantron. Her hands were shaking as she grabbed a pencil. *Wait it's Mackenzie Bishop. Grade? Technically a junior now but doing this for sophomore year? What was today's date? June 10...there was nothing special about that. What were the major themes of The Great Gatsby? Well, the representation of the American dream, old money versus new money, materialism, and technically racism considering Tom Buchanan's comments at the beginning of the book.* After writing her answer, Mackenzie found herself in a groove during the exam. Mackenzie's parents were eager to take her home after she breezed through the tests, realizing she knew more than she thought.

"What's the rush?" Mackenzie asked as they walked through the front door.

"SURPRISE!"

All of her high school friends jumped up to surprise her. Rachel, Serena, Michelle, and fellow trombones rushed up to her to hug her. Even her siblings, David, Esther and Mario, made it.

"We missed you so much," Rachel said.

"The last six months were so weird without you!" Serena exclaimed.

"Thanks, guys, I appreciate it," Mackenzie said. She looked around and noticed a "welcome home" banner decorated by her little siblings, who were now hugging her. Junie was at her waist, and Mikey was at her shoulder.

"Mackenzie, why are we holding the party now when you got back two weeks ago?" Junie asked loudly.

Rachel and Serena stared at her as her siblings went to get food.

"You got back early?" Rachel asked a little intensely.

"Yeah, my parents wanted an easier readjustment, and since you guys were taking finals, they didn't want me to get distracted." Mackenzie broke eye contact. "It's nothing personal."

Rachel nodded awkwardly as she headed over to the food table. She knocked over some stacked cups as she tried to grab one out of spite. Serena left her friends to check on her.

"You okay?" Serena asked.

"Just shut up," Rachel hissed. "We're at a party!"

"It's annoying, but it's what her family wanted," Serena said.

"Serena, leave me alone while I get food!"

Serena rolled her eyes and walked back to Mackenzie and Michelle.

"You're not going to believe what happened this semester, Mackenzie," Michelle said. "I got to watch Rachel play in St. Joseph's orchestra pit with her crush. We also all met at choir districts and North Central did better than St. Joe's."

"Yeah, I knew about Rachel and Mike's shenanigans this semester. By the way, is he here today?" Mackenzie asked as she looked around the front room.

"No, he's in New Jersey for the summer to catch up with friends," Rachel answered, restrained as she looked at her chips and guacamole. "We'll have fun without him."

"That's okay! I'm just ready to have fun this summer with you guys," Mackenzie said. "I finished my re-entrance exam, so hopefully everything is in order."

"But guess what," Rachel said, pushing her anger aside for excitement.

"What?" Mackenzie said.

"I'm going to need your help learning trombone this summer," Rachel replied. "I picked it up a few weeks ago for private tutoring since I'm getting bored with the oboe and it's really fun! I decided to sign up for community band at the local community college, and I know Mike is planning to do it too this upcoming semester."

"I'm so happy!" Mackenzie said. "I can't wait to help you! Hey, after the party, I could show you some notes. That's a great idea to get closer to Mike!"

Mackenzie and Rachel hugged each other. The girls went on to get drinks, eat cake, and constantly change Mackenzie's parents' playlist from 70s songs to show tunes.

A few weeks later, Mackenzie got her results from the exam, moving her into her junior year of high school. Everything was going to plan for her as the days passed quickly. After July melted away, Mackenzie prepared herself for band camp.

Chapter Twenty-Three

On the first day of band camp, Mackenzie was checking in with other upperclassmen as they stared at the new kids. She and saxophone player, Katie Sims, were exchanging section jokes when she saw a tall trim figure from the corner of her eye.

"How can you tell which kid is the trombone player on the playground?" Katie asked.

"How?" Mackenzie asked.

"He can't—" Katie got cut off.

"He can't swing and doesn't know how to use the slide!" Mike laughed loudly.

"Mike!" Mackenzie exclaimed as she hugged him.

"Hey, Mackenzie!" he cheered.

Mackenzie stared at Mike for a minute, taking in what she was seeing. He must have lost his excess weight because where she held him at his back was firm muscle now. His face was clear, and his hair was cropped high and tight.

"Holy crap! You look great!" she exclaimed.

"I know! My middle school friends and I did a fitness challenge this summer; we got really into it," Mike said. "I wanted to surprise everyone here with my transformation from ugly duckling to beautiful swan. I'm going to try to keep up my fitness to challenge my friends again next year."

"I like your hair, it's so short."

"I realized it was time to let the 'do go, and before you comment on my face, yes, I finally got around to actually using my acne medication."

"I'm so impressed," Mackenzie said. "Who are you trying to woo?"

"I want to woo myself," Mike said. "I'm the snack and a half that I deserve."

Mackenzie laughed at his comment before trying to take him in again. As she was staring at the new form of Mike, Drum Major Katie Birch called everyone in for introductions.

"Welcome new kids and welcome back everyone else," Birch said. "Get excited because this year's show theme is spies, so we're doing a lot of stuff from James Bond films."

Everyone showed appropriate enthusiasm until the groups broke off into respective sections. Mackenzie and Mike were now trombone leaders since they were upperclassmen. While new section leader Eddie Pohl scared the underclassmen with his passionate intensity, the two juniors made sure to check in on the younger students. Mike also felt himself cracking down on the new sarcastic kids to make sure the section was not subject to punishment hills. After a lot of sweat, sunburn, and a few hill runs due to mouthy sophomores, the marching band sounded better and better each day. After its final practice before the school year started Mike and Mackenzie were talking in the student parking lot.

"I'm actually a little nervous for Monday," Mike said.

"Why is that?"

"People are going to approach me and not recognize me."

"Because you're suddenly hot?"

"No, because of my giant scar and eyepatch."

"You'll be fine!" Mackenzie said. "At least you don't start taking AP classes Monday."

"That should be fun. Do you also have Mr. Sharpe for 2X?"

"Yeah!" They high fived.

"Do you have Miss Wilson again for 3Y?" Mackenzie asked.

"I think so. I know I'm taking AP Euro, English, Chemistry and Statistics."

"That's a lot of AP classes."

"Eh, it's less to take in college and looks good for college applications."

"That's true. Hopefully, we'll have lockers close to each other!"

"That'd be cool. I missed you last semester."

"I missed you too, Mike."

Mackenzie smiled before getting in her car.

Chapter Twenty-Four

That Monday, all juniors with driver licenses and parents willing to lend their cars excitedly met each other in the school's student parking lot. Rachel, Mackenzie, and Serena hugged each other near Rachel's nice, new sedan before heading into the school.

Just like Mackenzie and Mike hoped, they had homeroom together and lockers side by side. While filling her locker with books and the picture of her, Serena, and Rachel, the latter approached. Rachel watched her put up the old photo while thinking of something clever to say.

"My two-favorite people in one location!" Rachel chirped.

Mackenzie gave her a knowing smile.

"Hey, Rachel, how was your summer?" Mike said while unpacking. Rachel casually hugged him.

"It was all right. Work was tiring, but my family went to Maine for the Fourth of July, so I can't complain."

"That's fancy," Mike said.

"It wasn't that fancy; we didn't bring my dad's boat up there as we have in the past. Well, my locker is down the corner from you guys, but I'll see you later. Can't wait to catch up on your summer, Mike," Rachel said before walking off.

Mackenzie and Mike sat next to each other, in awe at Mr. Sharpe's mustache during their AP Euro class that day. Sharpe told his students he hadn't shaved it since 1982 and wasn't planning on doing so anytime soon.

"I wish I still had my mustache," Mike mumbled as the class got out.

"Only you miss it, Mike," Mackenzie informed him. "From the pics you've shown me, it does not compare to Sharpe's."

"Where are you off to?" Mike asked, heading down the other hallway.

"Lunch. I have religion next."

"Well, I'm off to AP Chemistry."

"Have fun!"

"I'll try my best. No promises."

Mackenzie found Rachel in the cafeteria and sat down with her. Before she could get a bite in, Rachel started asking her questions.

"What are your classes so far?"

"Mrs. Chalk for Algebra II and then I have AP Euro with Sharpe and Mike."

"You're so lucky you get to be with him. I think I have AP Statistics with him later."

"Yeah, but you don't want to hear Mike's rant about his former mustache."

"That's fine," Rachel said. "Also, did you notice how hot Mike got? I already liked him, but, damn, his new look makes me want him more."

Mackenzie laughed.

"All he's done is get buff. He's still Mike on the inside."

"Mike with a clear face and taking charge of his health. It adds to his personality," Rachel said. "It's like he's becoming more and more of my type as time goes on."

It was awkward talking about her guy friend's physical transformation with Rachel. Mackenzie wasn't jealous but was confused at Rachel's sudden lust for him. She zoned out to stop hearing her male friend be objectified until Rachel switched topics.

"Even if we don't have a lot of classes this semester, I'm glad he'll be in community band," Rachel said. "I'm a little nervous. We have our first practice next Monday. I know the coaching you gave during summer break will help me, but I hope he'll think I'm good at the trombone. I don't want to embarrass myself."

"Rachel, you can't embarrass yourself; this is Mike. He's non-judgmental."

"Well, while he's changed physically, let's hope his personality also hasn't changed."

Chapter Twenty-Five

Rachel had a great week because it went exactly how she wanted. She had AP Statistics with Mike on X days and lunch with him and his friends on Y days. She was also in AP English with him and Mackenzie. On top of that, she and Serena were seen as choir leaders now that they were upperclassmen.

Most importantly, Rachel woke up excited and ready to get to community band the next Monday. She waited and waited through classes until it was time to go to Central Community College's arts center. Her knuckles were white as she gripped her trombone case and walked into the band room. She introduced herself to others, including other high schoolers from the public schools, retired seniors, and some community college students. After a few minutes of searching, Rachel found the trombone section and planted herself in a seat nervously, clicking her feet on the floor.

"This seat taken?" Mike asked as he grabbed a chair next to her.

Rachel looked up.

"Yes, for my imaginary friend, Edward." She smiled.

Mike took his seat. "I didn't know you played trombone."

"I'm still learning it, but I hope I can play it as well as everyone else present. Mackenzie went on and on about how awesome it is, and she made it sound so intriguing, so I figured I would give it a try this summer after I got tired of the oboe."

After getting the sheet music, Rachel tried her best to follow along during rehearsal, but this instrument was harder for her. She wasn't hitting wrong notes on purpose, but playing in front of Mike was not making it easier. Rachel found herself apologizing profusely to Mike after rehearsal.

"I was paying attention to myself, so I didn't hear anything, but you'll get it in time," Mike said.

"Thanks." Rachel blushed.

"Have you done the Statistics problems yet?" Mike changed the subject.

"No, we just got them today, so I haven't had time yet."

"Okay, I had a question about problem twelve. I think I kept doing it wrong."

"Well now I know, I'll tell you all about it when I get to it."

When Rachel got home, she immediately began her homework after scarfing down dinner. After some reading for religion class, she opened her AP Statistics book and grabbed her notebook paper. The first few problems were hard, but the last five were somehow harder. After spending twenty minutes on question eleven, she got to question twelve. Rachel stared at the problem. She tried to find a solution but kept struggling with it. After twenty minutes, she gave up and texted Mike.

Rachel: I don't get 12 either :(

Mike: Welcome to the club! Have you talked to anyone else about it?

Rachel: Just you.

Mike: Do you have anyone else's contacts?

Rachel: Not really.

Mike: Should we just skip this question and complain to Mrs. Krammer next class?

Rachel: Yeah, but what if questions 13-15 are just as bad?

Mike: We'll just not finish them either

"Maybe I need a break :)" Rachel texted, implying she wanted to communicate more with Mike.

Mike: Lucky you. I think I'll have to work on my chem instead

Rachel: Okay.

Rachel gave up on Mike texting her back after staring at her phone for fourty minutes.

Chapter Twenty-Six

Rachel's life fell into its usual pattern of school, music, and sleep. She was excited every Monday to get to the community band where she would talk to Mike. This was in addition to texting him over homework problems and having lunches with him every other day. Having a routine was Rachel's favorite, but she also decided to shake things up by attending the school's home football games every chance she could. After every game, she and Serena would go to the band room and wait for Mackenzie and Mike. Every conversation usually ended with them casually mentioning taking Mackenzie back to Rachel's house for a sleepover. Rachel kept hoping Mike would invite them to a party where she could talk to him, but it never happened.

Rachel was about to give up on the idea when the girls were invited to an annual band party after a game in October. The party was near Mike's home, so Rachel was excited at the possibility of seeing it. The whole ride to the party, Rachel kept giving anxious looks to Mackenzie and Serena in the backseat of Shirleen while Mike talked and talked about AP Chemistry. After getting through the front door, Mike made a beeline to the cooler with non-alcoholic drinks. Rachel made a beeline to him.

"No beer tonight?" Rachel asked him.

"My parents are a few houses down," Mike said. "Also, this may not be my house, but tonight's house rule is don't spill alcohol on me. I don't want them to smell it and conduct an investigation."

"Well, that's going to make me want to do it to you now." Rachel laughed.

Feeling rebellious and trying to impress Mike, she decided to go to the beer table in the house's kitchen. No one followed her as she got lost in the crowd. Mike, Mackenzie, and Serena started talking to each other about the football game. After twenty-five minutes of talking, Serena decided to find Rachel, leaving the two friends to talk amongst themselves.

"How's the sports drink?" Mackenzie asked, feeling the need to keep the conversation going.

"You know how you can tell if it's spiked or not?"

"No."

"Yeah, I'm not sure," Mike said.

"It's bottled, man, it's not spiked."

"I mean look at the pit members with orange soda bottles, they're acting way too crazy to not have changed the labels on these. I'm blaming them if my parents catch alcohol on my breath."

"Pit members don't march. I don't trust them," Mackenzie joked.

"Do you trust me?" Mike asked.

"Well, you are my designated driver," Mackenzie said.

"Should I be your designated driver?" Mike replied.

"Well now I'm not drinking for the night," Mackenzie said as she put her cup of mystery punch down on an end table. "Do you trust me?"

"To cross the street without getting hit, no," Mike said. "To play well during halftime, yeah."

"I feel that burn pretty hard, Mike," Mackenzie deadpanned.

"I'm sorry. I didn't mean to hurt you," Mike said, realizing his comment was harsh. "But you're a good friend. I just feel like you're a bit of a danger magnet. Not just the car accident but how many times you tripped when we ran hills last year or the time you walked into Miss Wilson's door."

"Well, that's me, Mackenzie Joan Bishop," she said. "Also, those last two examples were your fault."

"I'll admit I caused us to run hills, but the door accident was your fault."

"You were talking to me and knew I wasn't looking at the darn door when I hit it! You didn't even warn me about it!"

"Well, you looked great with that head bruise for a week," Mike smiled. "Also, language, Mackenzie Joan."

"Thanks, I had named it Mike Jr. since you caused it."

"I'm the father of your former bruise? I'm honored."

"You're the mother too," Mackenzie said.

"I'm glad to be a parent already, but I don't want it to mess with my future," Mike quipped.

"What do you mean?"

"Well, not only for health reasons, but I'm just not interested in drinking anymore until I legally can. I heard my old freshmen friends have been arrested subsequent times for underage drinking. I just don't want to risk it. Colleges might not consider me with my infraction from ninth grade."

"That sucks, I'm sorry."

"Eh, I made my bad decisions early. I can only move forward."

About an hour later, Serena and Rachel came back.

"Sorry, I was stuck at the beer table forever!" Rachel interjected.

"Yeah?" Mackenzie asked.

"Yeah, some guy named Eddie was going on and on about how everyone getting drinks was sinning and breaking multiple commandments. He was trying to recruit everyone to go to confession tomorrow."

"It was really entertaining watching the Catholic guilt complex on twenty kids," Serena snarked.

"Yeah, I was arguing with him all this time, but how are you guys?" Rachel asked.

The conversations lulled back to small talk on the football game, pit band members, and homework due Monday. By one a.m. Rachel was back in her parents' house, grumpy after not living out her fantasy of drinking the night away with Mike and getting close to him like she was a year ago.

"Was I not being obvious with my flirting? He didn't even follow me to the kitchen," she complained to Mackenzie and Serena.

"Well, you didn't come back for one thing," Serena said. "I couldn't find you for almost thirty minutes because you excluded yourself at the beer table. You also didn't get electrolyte water to follow along with him."

Rachel ignored her friend's comments.

"What did you guys talk about when I left?"

"Mr. Sharpe's quarterly project and our thoughts on English monarchs. I then went to go get you," Serena said.

"Oh, so you and Mike were hanging out then?" She turned to Mackenzie. "Did you talk about me?"

"Just that you were gone for a long time," Mackenzie admitted. "We also talked about life in general. He was in a good mood to open up tonight."

"Did you say anything else about me?" Rachel said, hoping her best friends were her wing women for the night.

"Um yeah, I mentioned how hard you're working on trombone with me, and he said you've improved in community band," Mackenzie lied.

She felt terrible fibbing, but she wasn't even thinking of Rachel when she talked to Mike, she just didn't want to deal with her spiel of how slow they were moving or her gripes on how he hadn't realized he should love her yet.

"Well, thanks for saying that, Mackenzie. I really appreciate it!" Rachel perked up. "Today just feels like a disaster. Like I keep going two steps forward with Mike and then one step back."

"You'll get there," Mackenzie said, feeling herself drift off to sleep.

"He's just really great. Before we know it, we'll be graduating and I feel like now is the time to make strides or else," Rachel said. "I only have so much time in between classes, clubs, and homework."

"Don't worry, you'll get there." Mackenzie yawned, wishing sleep could hit her immediately.

Mackenzie appreciated Mike as a friend and wanted what was best for him too. So, if she was annoyed with Rachel's incessant obsession with him, should she still support the relationship? Should she help Rachel with something she could barely remember to do tonight or just forget it all and say she's on her own?

Mackenzie stopped worrying as sleep quickly hit her. Now if only her dreams were free of her friend and Mike.

Chapter Twenty-Seven

Mackenzie did the impossible by waking up at 8 a.m. that Saturday because she was ready to leave her friend's house. If she left, Rachel would be upset, but Mackenzie was ready to get out and go clear her head. Mackenzie deliberated her thoughts as she wandered into the Hoyt's kitchen. She opened their refrigerator to look for a quick breakfast before she could leave.

While staring at all the avocado mixes and non-dairy kinds of milk, Mackenzie thought back to the night before. Mike seemed to have fun regardless of whether he was talking to Rachel or not. As flirty as Rachel was trying to be, Mike didn't seem to respond. Rachel also seemed aggressive with her and Serena last night when it came to approaching Mike. When was it no longer fun to ship them?

Maybe it was just a dry spell with Rachel, like she needed a break from her before restarting their quest. Mike seemed like he didn't have a type and Rachel was a catch, but it didn't add up why they weren't together yet. It also seemed weird how friendly Mike was with her last night. He told her about his plans and wanting to remain sober until he could legally drink. Maybe the pit section changed the labels on the drink bottles after all.

"Don't let all the cold out of the fridge."

Mackenzie turned around and found Rachel standing there. She checked the clock to see it was already nine a.m.

"Morning, Rachel! I'm surprised you're up early!" Mackenzie said.

"As are you," Rachel replied. "I couldn't sleep. I'm too anxious about last night."

"It's okay," Mackenzie said. "I feel anxious too."

"Why?" Rachel said, confused.

"Well, you were bugging out last night and I wanted you to be okay," Mackenzie lied again.

"Thanks, I appreciate it," Rachel said. "I've just never had a crush on a guy before; I feel so crazy about it all."

"Crazy is normal," Mackenzie said. "If you didn't feel crazy, you probably wouldn't like him."

"That's true," Rachel said. "I just wish I knew for sure if he liked me."

"He probably does; you're a catch."

"Can you find out for me?" Rachel asked.

"Yeah, sure."

Mackenzie couldn't back out now. She was her friend, and she was curious about Mike's feelings anyway. Mackenzie felt awkward as Rachel hugged her.

"Thank you so much. You have no idea what this means to me."

"You're welcome." Mackenzie sighed quietly.

Chapter Twenty-Eight

Mackenzie was even more unenthused than she normally felt walking into school Monday. She was used to unpacking her books as Mike arrived at his locker and Rachel would show up five minutes later to use her as an excuse to talk to him. She didn't want to see either today.

So, Mackenzie unpacked her books as quickly as she could and walked at almost a running pace to her first class. *Don't look back, don't look back,* she thought to herself as she jogged away from her locker.

Mackenzie eventually had to face the inevitable when she got to A.P. Euro and Mike was already in his seat.

"Hey," Mike greeted her casually.

"Hey, how's it going?" Mackenzie said.

"Good. I didn't do the reading for today. What happens to Anne Boleyn? Does she stay married to Henry?"

Mr. Sharpe happened to walk right by when Mike made that comment.

"I sure hope you don't assume that on the exam, Mr. Sienkiewicz," Sharpe said.

The teacher started class, perfectly ruining Mackenzie's chance to ask Mike about Rachel. Then, after band practice that day, Mike approached Mackenzie.

"So, do you have any dinner plans tonight?" he asked.

"Yeah. Why?"

"Keep this quiet but Dave Fisher, Kevin Higgins, and I are going to dinner at the local hotdog place. They give out discounts to students. Want to come?"

"Sure!" Mackenzie said, forgetting her leftovers being saved at home.

So, Mackenzie followed Mike, Dave, and Kevin to Hot Diggity Dog. She forgot how fun the two sophomores were away from the whole section.

"Hey, Mackenzie, what do you think of the Sriracha dog?" Dave asked as everyone ate.

"So far so good," she said, taking another bite.

"We're thinking of making this a tradition every week. It's not too expensive, is it?" Mike asked Mackenzie.

"Not at all. I got some money from the settlement after the car accident and can easily afford this. Can your fit body afford it, Mike?"

"Hey, there are healthy choices here, and it's not like I'm done attempting fitness," Mike replied. "Hotdogs have protein, right?"

"Well, if they do, I guess we're all good then!" Mackenzie smiled.

As she and Mike walked to her car, they talked about the weekend.

"I think it was an okay party. I just had fun with you," Mike said.

"Same here! I think I'm over parties at the tender age of sixteen," Mackenzie said.

"So old, you're one foot in the grave. I'll see you tomorrow at band."

As she walked to her car, she forgot about Rachel's request.

Chapter Twenty-Nine

Mackenzie forgot to ask Mike what he thought about Rachel that night, and the latter forgot to inquire about it for the next few weeks. Rachel was feeling more secure about their relationship now that she and Mike were regularly texting about community band and AP Statistics. Mackenzie's mind was occupied with thinking about classes, band, and her family. Asking Mike about his feelings wasn't even on the back burner for her, more on the side counter next to a knife set. At her weekly dinner with Mike, Kevin, and Dave a few weeks later, she asked them what the point was of their weekly tradition.

"Well, we thought it was fun since Kevin's dad owns the place, and its stress relief from class and practice for us," Dave said.

"Yeah, it's also good to get wisdom from the great Mike SINK-ev-wicks," Kevin joked.

"That's All-Powerful Grandmaster Mike SINK-ev-wicks to you," Mike added.

"What advice do you really need from him?" Mackenzie asked. "He's not as all-knowing as you think."

"Don't lead them on to the truth about me, Mackenzie!" Mike exclaimed.

"Eh, just about being an upperclassman and stuff," Dave said. "Maybe the future."

"The future?" Mackenzie asked. "What do you mean?"

"Dave and I are thinking of the seminary," Kevin said. "And Mike has a few cousins who are priests, so we talk about it."

"No way, I didn't know you have priest cousins." Mackenzie turned to Mike.

"Yeah, they're both in New York, though, so I don't see them often," he said.

"But that's sweet," Mackenzie said. "Hopefully, I'm not interrupting anything coming to these."

"Not at all," Kevin said. "You add a female perspective, so it's fun. We like hearing from you."

"Okay, so two possible future priests and two upperclassmen go to dinner once a week and this is normal for you?" Mackenzie asked the group.

"Mackenzie, we're all in marching band. Even you know we're all weirdos," Dave said. "Just sit and enjoy Dave Dinner."

"Dave Dinner?"

"I suggested to Kevin and Mike that we do this weekly, so this tradition is my legacy," Dave said. "Without me, we all wouldn't be here."

"Well, here we are, thanks to you," Mike said. He held up his cup of water and said, "To Dave."

Kevin and Mackenzie held up their cups. "To Dave."

"To me," he said before drinking his orange soda triumphantly.

After dinner, Mackenzie went home, content from her weekly chat with the underclassmen and Mike. When she got to her room, she checked her phone to find multiple messages from Rachel ranging from "hey" to asking her about homecoming in a few weeks.

Mackenzie: Sorry, I was busy

131

Rachel: It's okay. Have you talked to Mike yet?

Mackenzie: About what?

Rachel: You know.

Mackenzie: I'm sorry it's been a long day, what was I going to tell him?

Rachel: If he likes me!

Crap. Mackenzie knew she dropped the ball and wasn't sure how to explain she forgot to ask Mike without upsetting her. She could lie, but that would add to her Catholic guilt complex. She could tell the truth and get angry responses from Rachel. Or she could not respond to the text and when asked about it the next day, say she had homework and passed out. Mackenzie went with the last option because she didn't feel like talking to Rachel about Mike. The next day at school, Rachel approached Mackenzie when she was at her locker.

"Hey, Mackenzie," Rachel said.

"Morning, Rachel," Mackenzie said.

"Why didn't you respond to my texts last night?"

"After I got home? Sorry, I had some English homework I really needed to do and then passed out at my desk."

"Oh okay," Rachel said, looking out for Mike who had yet to arrive. "I just want to know how he feels and don't want to ask Serena to ask Mike."

"Why not?"

"You know Serena can be blunt."

Rachel shuddered at the thought of her other friend's possible direct approach to getting answers. Maybe she would have to get the answers through others or by getting close to his sister.

"You know what, it's fine. You don't have to ask him now that I think about it," Rachel said. "He may catch on to my feelings easily. I'll think of something."

"Oh okay," Mackenzie said.

Rachel walked away, too impatient to wait for Mike to show up as Mackenzie gave a quiet sigh of relief.

Chapter Thirty

That Friday, Mackenzie and Mike high-fived each other as they got out of school early and onto a school bus. The football team was traveling three hours away for a game, and Coach Dobbs demanded the school bring the marching band for encouragement. That only meant sixty more kids leaving classes for the game. The football team was having an encouraging season and was trying to make a playoff push. Next week was homecoming, before its last two games of the season. If anyone outside the football team could encourage them, it was the school's marching band.

Mackenzie and Mike got on the band bus, putting their instruments in the rack above them. Katie Birch told everyone to have a buddy for the day so no one got lost on the other side of the state.

"Seat buddy!" Mike yelled as he sat down next to Mackenzie.

"I'm honored," Mackenzie said.

"Get ready for some terrible times." He laughed.

For the first hour of the trip, everyone was talking excitedly and looking out the window. In the second hour, most students started their homework and listening to music. By the third hour, everyone got distracted again. Mike and Mackenzie were playing UNO with Kevin and Dave.

"UNO!" Mackenzie yelled as Mike got down to one card.

"Damnit!" he yelled, picking up extra cards. "This means war, Mackenzie Joan Bishop."

"UNO already is war, Michael Jeremy Sienkiewicz," she replied.

"Woah wait, Jeremy is your middle name?" Dave asked. "I thought it was Bartholomew."

"I thought it was Aloysius," Kevin chimed in.

"What are we talking about?" saxophone member Kelly Trask asked in a nearby seat.

"Mike's middle name," Dave said.

"I thought it was Bartholomew," Kelly said.

"Same," Zane Smith pipped up.

"What? I was told it's Aloysius," piccolo member Taylor Camp said from behind Mike and Mackenzie.

"Who has the middle name Aloysius?" Katie Birch said from the front.

"Mike!" shouted Taylor. "But it sounds like it's fake. I think someone exposed the truth a few minutes ago."

"It was Mackenzie!" Dave yelled.

"Well, what is it, Bishop?" Katie yelled.

Mike stared at Mackenzie. He was never going to trust her with a secret again. At least a better secret than his middle name.

"I mean, he's right here, guys," Mackenzie told the whole bus. "You can ask him."

"Mike, don't lie to us this time. What's your middle name?" Katie asked.

"I'm not telling!" Mike yelled defensively.

The bus stopped just in time at the stadium, and everyone was too distracted by carrying their instruments and equipment to care about Mike's middle name anymore.

"Well, at least you didn't completely betray me," he said to Mackenzie as he got out of his seat.

"You should be happy no one looked at the band roster to just see it there," Mackenzie pointed out as she followed him off the bus.

"Well, now I'm doomed," he replied.

The band got off the bus and found themselves opposite the Bishop Burch Cardinals band. After unpacking and getting some food from concessions, they were ready to get out all their energy on the sidelines. The band performed without a problem and watched the game in suspense as the Lancers and Cardinals kept the score close. The band almost lost it when the Lancers caught an interception in the last minute and a half of the game and ran it in for a touchdown. The score ended 30-28 and as they left the stadium while being booed, the band couldn't help feeling part of the victory. Maybe Coach Dobbs was right about them.

After getting back on the bus at ten, everyone braced themselves for the long drive home. It started with the back of the bus playing mafia. Mackenzie and Mike wound up getting the mafia a few times, and Mike sold her out every time.

"Mackenzie is definitely in the mafia; she gets super defensive," he started.

"That's not true!" she said as her voice raised. "Why would I murder?"

"Because no one would suspect the nice kid, and you were in the mafia in the last game."

"It's not me!" her voice squeaked again.

Everyone still alive in the game voted Mackenzie out. After six rounds of the game, everyone in the back broke off into small groups.

"That's for exposing my middle name," Mike whispered to her.

"Oh, because Jeremy is such an important secret," Mackenzie snarked.

"I must keep my name protected."

"From who? Witches?" Mackenzie asked.

"Yes."

"That's not enough to justify selling me out. At some point when I was a townsperson or the nurse, I still got accused."

"That's your problem."

The two sat in silence for a few minutes. Mackenzie checked her phone and texted back her parents where she thought the bus was at the moment. Mike stared at the seat in front of them.

"Don't worry, we're still good friends," Mike said.

"Thanks for the reassurance," Mackenzie said while looking out the window.

"No, I really appreciate you," Mike said. "I mean it sincerely."

"I appreciate you too," Mackenzie said, facing him.

Mackenzie felt herself getting tired during the drive. She closed her eyes for a quick second but soon heard Katie Birch telling everyone to wake up and they were back at the school. Mackenzie woke up and found Mike asleep next to her, his shoulder digging into hers with his head lolled toward her. After telling him to get up five times, he finally opened his eyes, took both their trombone cases off the compartment above them, and handed hers back.

"This was fun," he said to everyone before getting off the bus and heading to his car.

Mackenzie agreed with Mike that she had fun, but there seemed to be something positive about him today. He was extra lively.

She liked it.

Chapter Thirty-One

Every student that Monday was excited about homecoming, especially the football team, cheerleading squad, and band after Friday's game. Due to scheduling conflicts with Carmel High School, St. Joseph's was hosting a homecoming festival Friday night, the game Saturday afternoon, and the dance that night.

"I suppose I could ask Mike to the dance at the festival," Rachel pondered over lunch Monday. "And just enjoy the day and then the dance without all the anxiety of being at the dance that night."

"That works. But why ask him the night before? Why not some other time this week?" Mackenzie asked.

"I just don't know if I can because I'm too nervous. Maybe hold me to it this Friday?"

"Yeah, all right."

Mackenzie smiled. She wanted what was best for her friend and looked forward to the dance.

"Just remember, if he says 'yes', you may be going to the dance with a cowboy."

"I think that's part of his charm," Rachel said. "He's a sweet g—" her words were cut off by a series of sneezes.

"Bless you a lot of times! Are you okay?" Mackenzie asked.

"Yeah, I don't know what that was," Rachel said.

Mackenzie and Rachel continued on with their conversation about Mike's wardrobe choices before heading off to classes. After school, Rachel sneezed some more at the lockers but figured she was having fall allergies. Tuesday, she felt the same sneeze attacks. Wednesday, Rachel felt fatigue and chills in addition to her running nose.

"I don't know why I feel like death," Rachel said at the nurse's office. "I got my flu shot a few weeks ago."

"Well, that's the issue," Nurse Palmer said. "There's two strands of the flu and one vaccine that prevents one. Honey, I'm sorry but you have the flu. You'll have to stay home for three to seven days. I'll call your parents."

"But homecoming is this weekend!" Rachel cried. "I need to go."

"You can't go if you feel down, honey. We need to prevent further contagion here."

"Okay," Rachel said with tears in her eyes.

Rachel was one of the first flu cases at the school, which spread rapidly. It seemed by Thursday there were fewer and fewer students. By Friday, everyone was worried the football game was going to be canceled and they wouldn't hold the homecoming dance. Only two of the football players seemed sick. Every student took Nurse Palmer seriously when she said to wash their hands frequently and cover their coughs and sneezes.

Mary Kate Love and other choir girls were carrying hand sanitizer with them and offering it to others at the sound of a sniffle. Many students looked around nervously every time someone mentioned the flu.

"People need to calm down," Mike said to Mackenzie during Sharpe's class. "You've either got it today or you'll feel it tomorrow. Washing your hands isn't going to prevent anything."

"Are you sure about that?" Mackenzie asked. "Rachel is dying right now and is upset that she can't go to the game or dance tomorrow."

"That's true," Mike paused. "Eh, she'll get over it. It's only high school."

"Yeah, but it's also the present. She lives in the moment and can't see too far ahead," Mackenzie said.

"Well, by the time this is all over, she can live in the present again," Mike said.

Sharpe cut them off with the day's lesson.

✱ ✱ ✱

That evening, the school's soccer field was transformed with outdoor booths, inflatable games, and a stage currently hosting cheerleader performances. Mike, Mackenzie, Dave, and Serena attended the festival together and played all the four-person games together.

After stopping for popcorn, Serena threw out the line, "I wish Rachel was here."

"Would she like this event?" Dave asked.

"Well, she likes school spirit events," Serena said, thinking about how Rachel was not into carnivals, inflatable games that knock people over, and overpriced fair food.

"She would like the live music by the strings and guitars class," Mackenzie said as she pointed out ten classmates setting up as the cheerleaders left the stage.

"I'm just hype for the game tomorrow," Mike said. "I'm glad I didn't get the flu," he said before sneezing loudly.

"Bless you," the three others yelled at him.

Serena looked around for hand sanitizer. "Are you sure you're okay?" she asked, fumbling through her purse for a small bottle.

"Yeah, I'll be great. I need to be at this game and then I'm going to bust some moves at the dance," he said.

"But can you really dance in all that ranchero gear?" Mackenzie asked.

"You just wait, missy. I'm going to show you all what a master dancer I am with my bolo tie."

Mike missed that opportunity when he woke up the next day with a temperature of 101.2 and body aches. His parents correctly self-diagnosed Mike with the flu and he was left sick on the couch while homecoming continued.

Two other trombone players, a bass player, and five pit members were also gone from the flu. Even two defensive linebackers and three wide receivers for the Lancers were out due to the spreading sickness. With the lack of players and motivation, the team lost to Carmel 28-7. No one felt good on Saturday, even if they weren't sick.

Mackenzie and Serena went to the homecoming dance that night, saddened by the loss and lack of classmates to have fun with. They stopped in their tracks when a slow song played after their favorite pop song, wondering if there were any available guys to dance with.

"Hey, Moore, Bishop," a guy's voice said.

They turned around to see junior wide receivers Lars Grant and Tom Jeffords approaching them.

"Moore, want to dance?" Lars asked.

"Sure, Grant," she said.

"Bishop?" Jeffords asked.

"Okay," Mackenzie said as she put her arms around Tom's neck. "So did your dates get sick?"

"Kind of, yeah," Tom said. "You?"

"Serena and I didn't have dates, but we were going to meet some friends here who ended up going down with the plague," she replied.

"I get that," Tom nodded. "So, can you believe Mr. Murphy going nuts in class Friday?"

"So unfair! No one touched his whiteboard!"

After the song ended, the girls reunited. They ended up interacting with some band members and had fun jumping up and down to rock songs and participating in line dancing. The newest pop song ended with a power 80s ballad at the end of the night. Serena was approached by Luke, who asked her to dance as friends as his girlfriend was sick. Mackenzie was alone for a minute when she heard another jock type yell, "Hey, Bishop!"

She was expecting Tom when second-string quarterback Ron Hitchcock approached her.

"Hey, do you want to dance?" Ron asked.

"Sure," Mackenzie said. "So was your date sick too?"

"No, I went alone. I don't like going to these things with dates."

"Same, it's a semi-formal, not prom," Mackenzie replied. "Sorry, do we have any classes together?"

"I sit behind you in Algebra II and Bioethics."

Mackenzie laughed out of embarrassment.

"I'm so sorry. I should have known that."

"It's okay, I'm usually asleep in those classes."

"Wouldn't Mrs. Chalk or Mr. Anderson wake you up?"

"That's the trick." Ron smirked. "I learned a few years ago how to sleep with my eyes open. Never gotten caught."

"Who wakes you up though?"

"The bell. One-time Miss Wilson did when my nap went too late and I was still sitting in her fourth-period class."

Ron then gave her pointers on how to nap without getting caught in class. Mackenzie laughed as the power ballad faded to an end.

"Well, this was cool," Ron said as he took his hands off her waist.

"Yeah."

"Can I get your number? You know, to get notes from you now that you know my secret."

"Sure! Let me see your phone."

After exchanging numbers with Ron, Mackenzie met up with Serena to drive back to her home for a sleepover. The girls agreed that while it's bad Rachel missed the dance, at least Mike missed it too, so they wouldn't have to worry about her getting jealous if any other girl approached him. Or that he had fun without her or if Mike asked any other girl to dance. Mackenzie was just surprised at how many notifications she received from Mike instead of Rachel expressing his frustration that he missed the dance. He was eager for a guy who tried to play cool, but maybe it was because he was coming out of his shell more and more with her.

"So, you and Ron seemed cute," Serena started as she drove back to her place.

"You think?" Mackenzie asked.

"Well yeah, he's tall, cute, the second-string quarterback, and he approached you, right?"

"You have a point," Mackenzie said. "I guess I've never noticed him until now. He seems pretty sweet."

"You don't need to fall in love with him now or anything. It just seemed cute seeing the two of you dance."

"You're right, but it might be a nice distraction from all this Mike and Rachel setting up," Mackenzie said. "It's so tiring trying to get two people who are right in front of each other looking eye to eye to ask the other out."

"Ain't that the truth," Serena replied. "I asked Rachel one day why she couldn't ask him out point-blank and she acted like I told her to flash him for attention or something."

"She embarrasses easily, and she doesn't handle forwardness well," Mackenzie said. "She mentioned it at our sleepover last Saturday."

"Last Saturday? Was I not invited to last weekend's sleepover?" Serena asked.

"Rachel said you were at the pro football game that night," Mackenzie said.

"The Ravens played on Sunday night; Rachel knew I was free for a sleepover. I told her."

Mackenzie and Serena sat in awkward silence for a minute. Serena drove the car right to her street as Mackenzie fiddled with the radio presets.

"It's like I almost want to tell her I can't help her anymore," Mackenzie said.

"Why not? Too direct to her?" Serena asked.

"Yeah, that and I think she really thinks she needs our help," Mackenzie said. "She seems desperate but has no way to get with him or anyone."

"That's true, but what if we helped her just when she asked for it?" Serena said. "Like do nothing, but if she says, 'Hey, help me come up with a text to send him' or 'Hey, let's do a double date', then we do. You got Ron Hitchcock's number and I think he would be happy to do something casual."

"That's a really good idea, Serena," Mackenzie said. "I just wouldn't want to lead Ron on."

"You can tell him it's just a double date. You're not marrying him if you ask him out."

"Fair enough, but should I tell him it's because I'm helping Rachel?"

"Mack, stop worrying about Rachel. How can we help a girl who's never been in a relationship if we've never been in any ourselves? If you are even slightly interested in Ron, shouldn't you go for it? He's attractive and it never hurts. He's a nice guy from what I've heard."

"So, I'm mainly helping myself in this whole situation meant for Rachel?" Mackenzie asked.

"Yes, don't burn yourself out for others. You gotta take care of yourself before you can help those around you," Serena said, parking in front of her house. "Maybe if we lay off helping them, they'll come together more naturally like a Thomas Jefferson Laissez-faire economy sort of deal. We've got to be democratic republicans."

"Sure, just show off your U.S. History skills after we finished that class," Mackenzie mumbled.

"It's all I'm good at," Serena joked. "I couldn't get Luke to ask me out, but I can get good grades. Point is, if it's meant to happen naturally, it will, and if Rachel needs us to interfere that badly, she'll approach us."

Mackenzie thought about what her friend had said. It was tiring thinking about a couple with potential who were not happening and trying her best to get them together. Mike was pretty flirty with her lately, but she wasn't worried about it since he hadn't asked her out to anything.

"You're right, Serena, let's promise to not interfere anymore unless they ask for help specifically," Mackenzie said as they walked into her friend's house.

"Yes!" Serena yelled. "Laissez-faire!"

Chapter Thirty-Two

Mackenzie unpacked her books that Monday with peace after her new resolution with Serena. Nothing was going to affect her today anyway as Mike was going to be out sick for the week. While finishing getting her books out of her locker, she found hands covering her eyes.

"Guess who?" Rachel said.

"Not Miss Wilson threatening me with extra homework?"

"Tada!" Rachel said. "I feel so much better."

They squealed and hugged each other. Rachel was too excited for a Monday; classmates going down the hall stared at her.

"He's not coming today," Mackenzie said as her friend looked at Mike's locker.

"I know," Rachel said. "He actually texted me Saturday saying he came down with the flu too. He blames me for it even though we hadn't seen each other Wednesday when I got diagnosed."

"I'm surprised you feel better already," Mackenzie said.

"Me too! But my parents go into a hyperactive mode when it comes to illness recovery, so us Hoyts get better sooner than the average person."

"Well, that's a special family talent," Mackenzie said, dazed by her excited friend.

"So how was the dance Saturday? And the game? I heard we lost terribly."

"It was pretty bad without our players and band members," Mackenzie said. "I was surprised we even scored. The dance was also strange; it looked like most people were taken out by the plague. So that meant more strangers forced to mingle with each other."

"That's what I figured. Did you dance with anyone?"

"Some football players. Ron Hitchcock asked me to dance with him for the last song and then we exchanged numbers."

"Cool! Are you guys texting?" Rachel asked.

"Not really. He texted yesterday that he had a good time Saturday." Mackenzie shrugged. "He's cute, but I'm not head over heels for him."

"Might be a prom date option."

"Sure."

The girls walked off to their classes before the bell rang. After school, Rachel continued the conversation of the dance with Mackenzie at Serena's locker.

"You know, it's kind of bad of me to say this, but I'm almost glad Mike didn't make it to the dance," she said. "I wouldn't like the thought of him dancing with other girls."

"What about us?" Serena asked her. "What if we danced with him?"

"Well, it's fine with you guys because you're my friends and I trust you. He also sees you as friends," Rachel said, annoyed.

"Dances don't mean romantic interest per se. Look at what happened to me and Luke," Serena said.

146

"Yeah, well, you and Luke clearly weren't meant to be. You're too smart for him, and he isn't as interesting as you," Rachel said.

"Rachel, I'm glad you like this guy, but aren't you worried you sound a little jealous saying this stuff? Mike is probably dying on his couch and is too tired to hold his phone right now."

Rachel remembered why she didn't talk about boys that much with Serena anymore. Her friend's blunt words hurt, and she didn't want to be wrong.

"He's sick but I'll message him tonight that I missed him at the community band," Rachel switched topics. "Is that too clingy?"

Mackenzie and Serena looked at each other.

"No, not really if you say something like, 'Community band was boring without you,'" Mackenzie said.

"That's a good idea! Thanks for the help, Mackenzie," Rachel said before walking away.

Chapter Thirty-Three

Mike returned the next week with the rest of the school's student population. Rachel was the most excited to see him back at school, making sure to text him and frequently swinging by his and Mackenzie's lockers in her spare time. The school, for the most part, went back to normal. Teachers had slowed class lessons to keep from continuing on with so many students out. Despite this, Mike, Rachel, and other students found themselves in half-hour, after school lessons for the next two weeks to catch up.

Rachel took advantage of all of the extra time she now had with Mike. From asking him if he wanted to do extra study sessions to hinting they should hang out after the upcoming community band concert, Rachel was on it with trying to get Mike's attention. Mike told his friends at Dave Dinner about how it was weird how friendly everyone seemed to be around him.

"Everyone at community band said they missed me, and AP Stats classmates keep offering me help in catching up," Mike said. "Rachel keeps saying that while it's bad we all got the flu, it's good because all of us are closely working together, which somehow makes us all better learners or something. I just need a break from everyone."

"You got your break from people while crying on the couch for eight days," Dave said. "You really dragged the flu out."

"No way, that was two days. My parents were just super cautious about me; that's why I was out so long."

"Okay, but Rachel was back after five days since her parents went into hyperactive hospital mode," Mackenzie piped up. "She is determined to get good grades for college admissions."

"Are you guys looking at colleges yet?" Kevin asked.

"A little," Mackenzie said.

"Not quite, but my family loves Loyola, so I'll probably apply there," Mike said.

"Really?" said Mackenzie "What do you want to major in?"

"Maybe the sciences. I like STEM," Mike said. "Probably not math so I can get AP Sadistics to count for college credit. What about you?"

"I think I want to go somewhere small where I'm not just a number," Mackenzie said. "As for a major, probably music, but it is hard to get into some college music programs."

"I feel like we should go to our guidance counselors. They keep emphasizing it at those junior class meetings."

"I think they get more into detail next semester," Mackenzie said.

"You know what I should do, just give up." Mike leaned back. "Go become a hotdog artist and live in the trash bin outside this place."

"That's too bleak. You know my dad would give you a place while you looked for open dumpsters, right?" Kevin said.

"That's comforting," Mike said.

As Mike and Mackenzie walked to their cars, Mike took extra hotdogs with him in a box for home.

"You're still training for that upcoming 5K, right?" Makenzie asked him.

"Yeah, why?" Mike said, ignoring the hotdogs he put on top of his car as he fumbled through his pockets for his keys. "Oh, because I'm staying in shape. Yeah, I'm giving these to my sisters when I get home since they're visiting."

"Oh, what are they here for?"

. "My parents' thirtieth anniversary," Mike said. "We're having a family reunion Saturday."

"Sounds like fun!"

"I hope it is," Mike said. "Hopefully no one gets drunk and starts a fight."

Mike got in his car. As Mackenzie got in her car and turned the engine on, she saw Mike forget one thing as he drove away. The hotdogs slid down the back windshield of his car, some of them unraveling and leaving a trail of chili behind him for the next fifty feet.

Mackenzie: Nice job, dingus she texted him before she drove away.

When she got home, she saw a ":(" text from Mike.

✖ ✖ ✖

Rachel laughed at Mackenzie's story the next day.

"That's so funny," Rachel said. "He's great at forgetting things. He's left dinosaur erasers at his music stand after community band practice before."

"It just goes to show that no matter how weird you can act, girls will still like you," Mackenzie said.

Rachel continued to laugh.

"He's a weirdo, but I appreciate his weirdness."

Rachel and Mackenzie walked to their separate classes before getting told they had to go to the auditorium for another college assembly. Mackenzie found herself with Rachel and Serena, waiting for the presentation.

"Juniors, we realize we're a little behind the curve with this, but we need to prepare you for college applications," vice principal McNelson began. "We will have some colleges touring here in the next few months. Please make sure to visit them. You will get excused tardies for attending them. Additionally, at your class registration for next year in April, we'll have the guidance counselors talk to you about your college plans. As a college prep school, we want you all to see how far you can go with applying."

Teachers started passing out pamphlets about college planning, financial aid, and scholarships as guidance counselor Mr. Adrian Nathanson talked about financial planning. Mackenzie looked at the pamphlets in her hands, hoping she could think of a way to pay for college. Her parents were making more money with her mom in a full-time position now, but she felt uncertain. If she wanted to save money, she would have to go further. She still had some money from the settlement after she was hit by a car, but that meant quitting Dave Dinners. She would also have to get a summer job this year, but would that still cover tuition?

Mr. Nathanson cut through her train of thought by also talking about financial assistance. "You need to apply through FAFSA; they will help. You can also take out loans."

Mackenzie rolled her eyes. She saw the amount of her parents' student loan debts which they finally paid off two years ago.

After the lecture, Mackenzie went back to class and then had lunch with Rachel.

"So where do you want to go to college?" Rachel asked.

"I don't know. I haven't really thought about it that much," Mackenzie said. "I think I want to go into music, but that's about it."

"Well, there are college search websites with filters to help you there," Rachel said. "Personally, I want to go to Cornell and major in physics."

"Why do you want to go to Cornell?" Mackenzie asked.

"My family has always loved Cornell. They have a beautiful campus. The academics are good too. My grandfather went there and used to tell me stories about it when I was a kid. They were so enchanting. It's also large enough so I won't feel like I'm a big fish in a small pond."

"You think you're that special here?" Mackenzie asked.

Mackenzie was genuinely surprised her friend not so humbly called herself a big fish at a school with a population of over 800 and climbing. Usually Serena called Rachel out, but now it was her turn to speak up.

"Special? No, not in a bragging way, but I think I'm at least in the top five of our class, which is good since I need that edge to get into Cornell."

"Are you going to apply to any other schools?"

"Loyola, Georgia Tech, Carnegie Mellon, and Boston University."

"Those are all pretty diverse."

"Yeah, but they're all good schools," Rachel said. "I feel like I have a good chance of getting in to them. You really need to test yourself, Mackenzie, to see what kind of college you want and what you'll get in to."

"I know. I'll do it after school," Mackenzie said as she felt herself drawing away from the table.

"Hey, are you still coming to the community band concert Sunday?" Rachel asked.

"Yeah, I'll make it," Mackenzie said as she walked away at the sound of the lunch bell. Rachel was really sure of herself to announce she was getting into esteemed schools. It shouldn't have bothered Mackenzie, but it did. She used to think Rachel was haughty on the surface but hadn't seen this attitude since freshman year.

That day after marching band practice, Mackenzie and Mike started talking about the lecture the whole junior class sat through.

"I still want to go to Loyola," Mike said. "But I should look at other places. My other sister you haven't met, Mary, went to Boston College. I may look at it. It's also Catholic."

"That's cool," Mackenzie said. "It's like everyone knows what they're doing, and I don't know what I want. And I know, I know, I should search colleges, but I haven't had the time yet. I'll do it tonight."

"Well, let me know when you search so we can text."

✺ ✺ ✺

That night after breezing through homework, Mackenzie found a college search website.

Mackenzie: I'm on it, she texted Mike.

Mike: Any colleges yet?

Mackenzie: No

Mackenzie went to the option for major searches and clicked arts and humanities, feeling hopeful that was what music was under. She typed in "music, general" in a second search bar just to be sure. She then went to the financial tab and dragged the bar to see if she can have on one hundred percent meets her financial needs. She clicked on a work studies program box and entered her results. *Three hundred sixty-three results. Not bad,* she thought to herself.

Mackenzie: 363 options

Mike: Is one near Chicago?

She clicked the Illinois state tab and found twenty-one.

Mackenzie: Plenty. Our friendship will stay strong

Mike: Then my work is done

Mackenzie clicked on the first option, the University of Chicago. It's out of state tuition was more than $60,000, but the average financial aid package was $57,900. She saved the result to her web browser to keep in mind. Mackenzie spent the next two hours looking at colleges before falling asleep on her laptop, satisfied there was some hope for her after all.

Chapter Thirty-Four

Mackenzie was running late Sunday to Mike and Rachel's community band concert. The community college was twenty minutes across town, and she got back late from Sunday Mass because her parents kept talking with everyone at coffee and donuts afterward. She didn't change out of her church clothes, but her parents kept saying they wanted to talk to her about applying for college at some point. *And we're going to have a serious talk, just not today,* Mackenzie thought as she ran through the house.

As Mackenzie ran out the door, she realized she left her driver's license in her second purse, ran all the way upstairs, found it, hurried downstairs, and jumped into her car, which had its gas light come on as soon as she started the engine. After getting gas, Mackenzie seemed to hit every red light in town.

She ended up at the concert ten minutes late and prayed the college's auditorium was not brightly lit. She crept in the back before seeing the open seat Serena saved for her in the dimly lit auditorium.

"Thanks," she whispered to Serena as she quietly sat down.

"No problem."

They sat and watched the band perform for an hour. The band sounded beautiful, and their hard work showed. The girls were surprised when the band went from playing a Mozart requiem to modern pop, and they took part in a standing ovation at the end of the concert.

Mackenzie and Serena hugged their friends during the reception.

"I'm so glad you guys made it!" Rachel said. "We had a blast rehearsing."

"Yeah, I liked your modern songs," Serena said.

"Yeah, and 'Sleigh Ride' was cute too," Mackenzie added.

"Did you like anything from the beginning?" Rachel asked.

Serena covered for Mackenzie, saying she liked "Flight of the Bumblebee" even though she arrived two minutes into that song. Rachel nodded and moved on.

"So, Mike, what was your favorite part about all of this?" Rachel asked him.

"The cake we get at the end of it all," Mike said as he downed a corner piece.

Rachel and Mackenzie laughed.

"I also liked the requiem we played because I am a dark, twisted individual," he added.

"Aren't we all?" Rachel said. "We are taking AP Sadistics after all."

"Ugh, don't make me think about tomorrow's homework," Mike said. "Mrs. Krammer, that woman, is trying to kill me."

"She's trying to kill all of us," Rachel agreed.

Rachel continued talking one-on-one with Mike. Serena and Mackenzie stared at each other as they tried to join the conversation.

"So, AP Euro is fun," Serena casually started. "I like how we remember Henry's wives as divorced, beheaded, died, divorced, beheaded, survived."

Mackenzie nodded to her friend as she got annoyed at Rachel's antics. But Rachel kept just facing Mike, getting more and more animated about math class.

"Yeah. Anne of Cleves was my favorite wife of Henry. What about you guys?" Mackenzie asked to deaf ears.

Five minutes later, Mike made his way out of the concert hall.

"Well, that went well," Rachel said. "We got him to talk."

"Mainly to you," Serena pointed out.

"He was talking to all of us. I just jumped in to keep the conversation going."

"With topics only y'all are involved in," Serena said. "We're not stupid just because we aren't taking AP math, Rachel."

"What's your problem? You guys know I like him, and you both ship us," Rachel said.

Mackenzie kept her head down the whole confrontation. For one thing, she agreed with Serena, but for another, she didn't want to upset Rachel.

"We do, but we also want to spend time with both of you. We came here to see you guys perform and then interact with you both, not watch you alienate him in front of us awkwardly."

"Well, you didn't have to come! I was planning on flirting with him here anyways."

"Well, I guess I wasted the time I would have used to study for my algebra test tomorrow to come here and watch the blandest flirting I've ever seen," Serena said. She threw her paper plate in the trash and left.

"Can you believe her?" Rachel turned to Mackenzie. "I thought I was doing what everyone wanted."

Mackenzie awkwardly nodded. "Serena hasn't seen much of you this semester other than choir, so that's probably why she's being like that."

"Well then maybe she should say something to me before she blows up," Rachel huffed before heading out.

Mackenzie stood there zoning out for a few minutes before realizing what happened. Her friends had another confrontation, with Serena being right but both of them insanely stubborn. Mackenzie didn't want to interfere. She decided to avoid her phone for the rest of the day so she didn't have to see either's angry texts and be expected to respond.

Chapter Thirty-Five

Grudges came and went for the next few weeks as Mackenzie tried to stay out of her friends' drama. Thankfully, it was near the end of the semester and everyone dropped their anger for finals and midterms.

Mackenzie, Dave, Mike, and Kevin were having their last Dave Dinner of the semester that Wednesday before finals week. After the football team's playoff hopes ended early, the four decided to carry on the weekly tradition for fun. Mackenzie was laughing with her friends when she realized she had to tell them she would have to quit participating in their weekly ritual.

"I don't know what I'm going to do without you guys, but I need to save money for college starting two weeks ago." Mackenzie sighed. "This will be my last Dave Dinner."

"No!" Dave yelled.

"It's okay, Mackenzie. Well, it's okay everybody," Kevin said. "I talked to my dad, and since we've brought in customers by just sitting at the window for dinner and being lively, you guys don't have to pay anything for Dave Dinners ever again."

Mackenzie and Dave cheered while Mike's jaw dropped.

"Why didn't you tell us sooner?" Mike asked. "I also could have saved money for college."

"Well, my dad and I talked about it yesterday, so," Kevin replied. "Just enjoy this as the last paid dinner here."

"No, I want a refund!" Mike jokingly yelled. "Refund! Refund! Refund! Refund!"

Mackenzie and Dave joined in until they saw other customers staring at them.

"So how are finals looking for you guys?" Dave asked the juniors.

"I think I can manage Sharpe's exam and Miss Wilson's, but I need to study for Algebra II," Mackenzie said.

"My mom said if I don't get a B on the AP Stats midterm then I can't go to our Boston band trip this spring," Mike said.

Everyone stared at him in horror.

"Are your grades okay?" Mackenzie asked.

"Grades don't have feelings, Mackenzie," Mike snarked. "But yeah, this semester was hard, and if I get below a B on the midterm, it's going to pull down my GPA. My parents think by threatening me over grades it's going to help me study harder and get into better colleges."

"That's...rough," Dave offered. "Isn't AP Statistics weighted? Wouldn't a B still be an A in that class?"

"Yeah, tell that to my parents," Mike nodded. "They say it's for the good of my future."

The band held a class trip every other year to a big city where they would perform at a large concert hall and tour the area. Mackenzie missed the Atlanta trip her freshman year but had saved some money from occasional babysitting, gifts from extended family, and some of her settlement money that she sectioned off from her college fund for this trip. Mike was ready to experience what made these trips so great that other band members would always seem to go on about.

Mike was confident he could pass the AP Statistics exam, but the pressure to excel was getting to him. The next day at AP Stats, all of the students gathered together for a giant study session. Afterward, Rachel offered to host a study group at her house for everyone. Tim Daniels, Leah Walters, and Lauren Loesel agreed. Rachel kept hoping Mike would volunteer to go to her house, but he seemed to ignore her encouraging invitations. One night while doing math homework, Rachel finally had enough and decided to text Mike.

Rachel: Hey, need any stats help this weekend?

She second guessed her text as it sent.

Mike: Can't. Parents are taking me to the philharmonic concert Saturday, and Sunday is band service day.

Rachel: Oh. Maybe another time after school we could study together and organize a group.

Mike: Sure

He then he put down his phone and stared at practice questions.

Mike: I don't get problem 14. Do you?

Rachel: Yeah. Don't look at the problem as a categorical variable but as a quantitative variable.

It took Mike ten minutes but he got it.

Mike: thanks

Rachel held her phone in her hand, grateful she got some recognition from Mike. Maybe he wasn't bluffing about doing an after-school study session. That Monday, Mike approached Rachel about a study group.

"Can we still do it?" Mike asked. "Form a Statistics study group? Maybe tomorrow before finals?"

"Yeah!" Rachel said enthusiastically. She hurt her neck a little when she turned her head quickly to face him.

"Great, let me text everyone to meet us in the library tomorrow." Mike pulled out his phone. "Three thirty work for you?"

"Uh huh!" Rachel said, high-pitched. "I mean, yeah, that should be enough time to assemble everyone."

✱ ✱ ✱

Ten classmates joined their study session, to Rachel's internal chagrin. But at some point, Rachel got used to Mike acting oblivious; she took it as one of his many charms. Leah and Lauren later thanked Rachel for the help after the session, but that gratitude barely supplemented her need to just study with her crush.

Finals came and went like a rollercoaster at St. Joseph's. Everyone in Mrs. Krammer's AP Stats felt like the test was easier than it should have been, yet also were relieved it was one less stressor before the holidays. Rachel and Serena seemed to forget their feud and exchanged Christmas gifts with Mackenzie. Serena gave them Christmas ornaments with their initials painted on a bulb. Mackenzie gave her friends scarves crocheted by her mom.

Rachel made sure to give her friends their gifts separately so Serena wouldn't get jealous, giving her a bracelet and Mackenzie a BFF necklace shaped like a heart with a musical note. Mackenzie got the back half that read "st ends."

"I like it," Mackenzie said as she put Rachel's gift around her neck by her locker.

"I'm never taking mine off, " Rachel said. "You have been so amazing and so helpful since I met you. I can't imagine a greater friend."

Mackenzie laughed as Rachel stared at her, taking a few seconds to realize she was serious.

"I don't know about that."

"No, thank you for the help with Mike," Rachel went on. "You've helped me so much with trying to get close with him. I've never had a serious crush like this and I'm so thankful to have you as a confidant. We're going to make a lot of progress with him next semester."

Mackenzie awkwardly smiled at her friend as Rachel gave her a hug. While she wasn't into Mike anymore, she was just secretly done with shipping her friend with Rachel. She wondered if Benedict Arnold ever felt as much guilt as she.

Chapter Thirty-Six

Everyone came back from winter break relaxed except for the band kids who were getting more excited about the Boston trip day by day. Students began counting down as soon as they got back even though the trip wasn't until spring break in early April.

Mike proudly told everyone he got a perfect score on his AP Stats exam to remind them that he's brilliant. He made sure to yell his grade in the hallway when someone mentioned the exam. Everyone was so over it by day two of the semester that Mrs. Krammer even threatened to lower his exam to an eighty nine before the semester was over because she could if she wanted. Mike finally shut up.

Time seemed to speed up for the school's upperclassmen that semester. Mackenzie, Rachel, and Serena found themselves hating their AP classes as they started reviewing what they already learned in addition to continuing lessons. Rachel was scheming once again with Valentine's Day carnations and joining the spring musical's orchestra pit for *Beauty and the Beast*. Without needing a ride home and only talking to Mike for about five minutes after rehearsals,

Rachel felt unlucky leaving practice on St. Patrick's Day. The closer they got to the band's spring break trip, Mackenzie's praying got more and more intense during Lenten Stations of the Cross every Friday.

After Easter Sunday Mass, Mackenzie and the rest of the band was outside of St. Joseph's and getting into a commercial bus. Mackenzie found herself toward the middle and placed her backpack next to her so no one would sit by her. It was selfish but useful for these long trips. Mackenzie had her earbuds in and music playing on her phone when she sensed a figure staring at her in the aisle. *Hopefully, no one is trying to get a seat.*

"Too bad," Mike said as if reading her thoughts. He put her backpack in the overhead compartment and sat down next to her. "Hi, I'm your seat buddy, Antonio."

"Hi Antonio, I'm Regina." She shook his hand without taking out her earbuds.

Mackenzie continued listening to music as the band's bus started heading out to Boston. A few hours into the trip, Mike started prodding her with small talk.

"But I have the best Easter story to tell, so you need to tell yours first," Mike insisted.

"Fine. It was nice. Esther, Mario, and Mary Grace visited, and we had a quick dinner before I got here," Mackenzie said. "I don't get what could happen in the span of six hours this morning to be so exciting for you."

Mike started laughing. "During the homily, the priest went 'When Peter said' and someone's phone went off with the ringtone being a woman's voice saying, 'Pick up the phone, bitch!'"

Mackenzie and Mike started laughing together. Mike then went into how his sisters attend church with his family and how they always had lamb cake. Mackenzie listened intently before they started playing with trivia cards with classmates for the rest of the trip. Once the busses stopped at the hotel on the outskirts of Boston, everyone unloaded their bags in their rooms before dinner.

Chaperones broke up the groups into sections to wander around, so Mike and Mackenzie found themselves talking with each other and Eddie Pohl around Boston harbor.

"Do you think there's still tea in there?" Mackenzie joked.

"Want to try it?" Mike said. "I bet it doesn't taste like fish poop."

"You can't do that!" Eddie yelled. "Why did I get paired with you weirdos? Don't drink the water!"

Mike and Mackenzie ignored him and continued making jokes about tasting the harbor's water.

"If you had to throw Dave or Kevin in here, which one would you throw?" Mike asked.

"I don't think Kevin can swim," Mackenzie replied.

"So definitely him then."

✖ ✖ ✖

The next day, the band got out their equipment and headed to Boston Symphony Hall to rehearse. After hours and hours of practice, Mrs. King let the students wander around the city for two hours. Mike, Mackenzie, Dave, and Kevin went with a group of students to walk around Harvard's campus.

"Do you guys want to apply here next year?" Kevin asked them.

"Not really," Mike said.

"Nope," Mackenzie replied.

"Really?" Kevin asked.

"Why would I apply?" Mackenzie said. "I don't think they're music-oriented for one think. Also, the school's acceptance rate is impossibly low."

"It's too snooty for me," Mike said. "But I'll apply if you'll apply, Mackenzie."

"Sure, why not waste fifty dollars on another college application while my family struggles financially," Mackenzie snarked. "If I pay for your souvenirs here, will you pay for my application?"

"Sounds like a plan," Mike said as they shook hands. "But know that I want matching Harvard socks to go with my Harvard underwear... Hey, want to sneak off for a bit? My sister Mary introduced me to a really good lobster roll place nearby a few years ago?"

"Won't we get in trouble?"

"The chaperone won't notice if we go for fifteen minutes. Hey, Kevin, text us where the group is in fifteen," he said.

"Okay," Kevin nodded.

Mackenzie and Mike sneaked away from the group quietly and were in front of a lobster roll place in seven minutes. Mike ordered them rolls to go and texted Kevin to know where their group was, which was moving to the school of engineering.

"So, I'm not picky, but this lobster roll tastes okay," Mackenzie said as they walked back to Harvard. "Why do you like it?"

"A few years ago, I visited Mary when she was working in Boston and she took me here for a fun night, so I like it."

"That's very sentimental of you."

"I can be that sometimes," Mike said, making a face as they joined the group again.

No one seemed to notice they were gone until Eddie Pohl turned around and asked Mike and Mackenzie where they got food.

"The food cart outside that one hall that we saw obviously," Mike said, taking a bite of his roll.

Mike's shenanigans didn't seem to stop as he would distract Mackenzie with funny faces during rehearsals. Mackenzie was so distracted by his faces, she hit the wrong notes a few times and made Mrs. King restart some songs over and over.

That evening, the band met for dinner and Mike sat next to Mackenzie. The band made sure to take its time in Boston, touring all the sights. Mike remained by Mackenzie's side for the most part, which surprised her.

✖ ✖ ✖

That night after touring the Freedom Trail, they performed to a crowded room, filled with family members and people free on a Thursday.

After a great show, the band loaded the bus to drive home. Mike and Mackenzie sat together again. After a few hours Mike drifted off to sleep, but Mackenzie was still alert. Saxophone Mary Lowe turned around from the back of her seat and whispered to Mackenzie.

"Hey, what's the deal with you and Mike?" she asked.

"What do you mean?" Mackenzie replied.

"Are you guys dating?"

"No, he's just a friend."

"Are you sure?"

"Yeah, I really don't see him that way. He's more like an annoying brother," Mackenzie said.

"Oh okay," Lowe said before turning around. "You guys would make a cute couple."

Mackenzie froze as she thought about what Mary said. She didn't see Mike as anything more, but what was with his behavior this week? Mike was flirty and was super attached to her this week. But she excused all of it as him being a good friend. Mackenzie couldn't sleep now as she thought of her friend's intentions for the week. As elusive as Mike was, wouldn't he be forward in his intentions with her? Mackenzie was still lost in thought as the bus came to a stop.

When she got off the bus at four a.m., a wave of tiredness hit her. Thankfully, Esther was there to take her home.

"How was the trip?" Esther asked.

"It was good," Mackenzie said.

"Hang out with anyone?"

"Mike mostly."

"Mike? Is that guy I told you not to date?"

"I don't care. We're just friends," Mackenzie said sternly as she buckled her seatbelt.

Chapter Thirty-Seven

Prom became the next frenzy for the upperclassmen at St. Joseph's. Students without a date had a month to get someone or else go alone to the grand dance. Underclassmen hoped to be asked by upperclassmen to get in while all the single juniors and seniors zoned out during classes thinking of who to ask.

One sunny day in April, Rachel and Mackenzie were sitting at lunch, trying to make plans for the event. Serena had a date with Luke Jackson as totally platonic friends, as he told her after his girlfriend broke up with him a few weeks ago for a lacrosse player. Rachel wanted to ask Mike but wasn't sure how to go about it.

"I mean, now is the time to express your feelings if you want to go with someone," Mackenzie said.

"Yeah, but I don't know how to just walk up to him in the hallway and ask," Rachel said. "Like, 'Hi, Mike, you are a cool person. Will you go to prom with me?'"

"That's perfect," Mackenzie said. "Do something specifically like that, or during your math class or something."

"I could do that," Rachel paused. "What about you? Are you going to ask anyone to the dance?"

"Not really. I don't like anyone here romantically."

"What about that guy you exchanged numbers with?" Rachel asked. "The guy from homecoming? Ron something?"

"Ron Hitchcock? I haven't even texted him," Mackenzie said. "He's only reached out to me at Thanksgiving, Christmas, and Easter."

"Which are all holidays, meaning he wanted you to know he was thinking about you away from school," Rachel added. "What about Valentine's Day? Did he send you a carnation?"

"It's not like that," Mackenzie said. "I mean, he did send me a carnation, but...oh, okay. I see what you mean."

Rachel laughed at Mackenzie. Here she was standing right in front of Ron and didn't realize he had feelings. Sounded familiar. Maybe too much like her and Mike, but that relationship would hopefully come to fruition soon.

"It won't be as fun if Serena and I have dates and you go alone," Rachel said.

"Yeah, I get it. I'll ask him when I see him."

Mackenzie made an effort to look for Ron in her religion class after that conversation with Rachel. He slugged into Mr. Anderson's classroom and took a seat in the back corner with two of his friends. She realized she was staring at her classmate when he waved at her, so she awkwardly waved back. After sitting for ninety minutes of class, Mackenzie got up and made an effort to get to Ron's desk.

"Hey, are you still sleeping?" She poked Ron.

He immediately moved his arm.

"Ow, what the heck, Bishop?" He got up.

"Sorry! I was just thinking about what you said at homecoming," Mackenzie rambled.

"Shhh, that's an open secret," Ron said.

"Anyways," Mackenzie said. "Will you go to prom with me?"

Ron stared at her.

"I mean as friends. We don't need to date or anything."

"Sorry, but I already have a date," Ron replied. "Leah already asked me out. But maybe I'll see you there."

"Yeah." Mackenzie walked away feeling awkward from the whole interaction.

During AP Statistics that day, Rachel turned around in her seat to talk to Mike while working on homework. Everyone was chatting casually while Mrs. Krammer graded quizzes. Mike was buried in his work.

"So, prom," Rachel started as her heart pounded. "Are you going?"

"I don't know," Mike said. "Tickets are expensive."

"Not if you have someone go with you; the couple's rate is way cheaper."

"True, but where will I find someone?" Mike asked.

"I'm available for prom," Rachel mumbled.

"I would be a boring date to whoever went with me anyway," Mike said.

"I bet you wouldn't be," Rachel said. "It would be fun to go."

"I don't know if I'm a prom person," Mike said as the bell rang.

He got up and went to his fourth-period class. Rachel wasn't quite sure if she even asked Mike out or if he realized he rejected her.

✦ ✦ ✦

The week of prom, Mike and Mackenzie found themselves griping at Dave Dinner about the dance.

"I mean, I put myself out there, but everyone is taking someone in the junior class," Mackenzie said. "I even asked out Ron and he's taking Leah Walters. So now Rachel, who is also dateless, is insisting we buy tickets together to save money. And she also wants to take us in a limo, but us and Serena and Luke Jackson can't pool all the money together for that."

"I don't want to go to the prom. I don't see the big deal with these dances," Mike said. "It's going to be awkward watching our classmates grind in front of the teachers."

"You're assuming that," Kevin said. "Also, doesn't that mean both of you guys are dateless for the prom?"

"Yeah, why?" they both asked.

Mackenzie saw where the question was leading and, knowing the rumors about her and Mike that were spreading around the band, tried to shut it down.

"Hey, now that I think about it, Kevin, what are your plans for Saturday?" Mackenzie asked.

"Help my dad with the store during the day."

"So, will you go to prom with me then?" she asked him.

Kevin was surprised. "Sure!"

"No, Mackenzie, you have to do an official promposal." Mike insisted. "Get down on one knee!"

"Kevin Matthew Higgins, will you go to prom with me?" Mackenzie said on one knee with a French fry in her hand. Kevin took the fry.

"YES! I accept!"

Dave and Mike applauded as other patrons stared at the table.

"Hey, if Rachel is dateless too, maybe she should take Dave," Mike suggested.

"Or you could take her," Dave replied.

"I don't want to go to prom," Mike insisted. "But now that we have our table's official prom couple, what color dress are you going to wear, Mackenzie?"

"Either this purple one I have from a few years ago or a black and white dress I'm borrowing from my sister," Mackenzie said.

That night after dinner, Mackenzie texted Rachel about a change of plans for prom and gave her Dave's number. Rachel would be happy to take Dave and now they didn't have to split tickets together and watch other couples dance the whole night.

***

As sad as she was that Mike wouldn't attend, Rachel was ecstatic for prom. She and Dave had been texting about matching her dress's color with his suit tie and where to meet everyone.

Her head was in the clouds until she was called into the front office the day before prom. Her parents sat in the vice principal's office, looking solemn.

"We're so sorry, Rachel, but Grandma Clarice died last night," her father said.

"What?" Rachel asked, shocked.

"We're leaving now for the funeral in Maine and to look over her assets," her father said.

Chapter Thirty-Eight

Rachel missing prom was only the start of the day's troubles for Mackenzie's prom group. Kevin texted Mackenzie saying his father was making him work the night shift at the restaurant even though it was prom because he had two more years to attend. So, Dave and Mackenzie texted each other at noon and decided to be each other's dates. Makenzie, Dave, Serena, and Luke met outside a family restaurant for dinner before the big dance. The guys gave the girls corsages, and everyone made sure to take lots of pictures for their family and social media.

When Luke got up from the table during dinner, Dave started asking Serena questions.

"So, you guys are still not dating?" Dave asked.

"No, but also at this point Luke is about to graduate, so what's the point of dating if he's just turning around for college in August?" Serena said. "I'm just glad he still wants to be friends."

"Fair enough," Dave said.

After dinner, the group went to the local community college's ballroom for the prom. Girls hugged each other and took photos,

Serena twirled around in her sparkly light blue ball gown, and Mackenzie showed off the details of her white dress with black lace after taking off her shawl at a table. The skirt of the latter's dress kicked out at the knees, and when she looked around and saw classmates stare at her, Mackenzie was grateful to have an older sister to lend her clothes.

Five minutes into the DJ playing tunes, everyone was on the dance floor. The group was having a good time, and after the first slow song finished, Mackenzie and Dave turned around to a voice saying, "You started without me?"

"Mike!" they both shouted. Serena and Luke turned around to face him.

"Hey, guys," he said to the whole group. Mackenzie was shocked for a few seconds. Not only did Mike decide to go but he also wasn't wearing his usual bolo tie and blue shirt. Mike made a conscious effort to wear a fitted black tuxedo with a white dress shirt and purple bow tie. He made sure to comb his hair, which was styled, and wash his face before showing up. He was stunning.

"What?" he asked everyone as they were still staring.

"You came!" Mackenzie yelled.

"Yeah, I figured why not, you know? I could be dead before the next one," Mike deadpanned.

No one spoke again.

"But also, you guys made it sound like fun."

Mackenzie and Dave hugged him, and he joined their group for the night. During the second slow song, Dave told Mike to ask Mackenzie to dance, which he obliged. Mackenzie and Mike danced as he had his hands around her waist and hers around his neck. Neither of them talked for thirty seconds.

"So why did you come tonight actually?" Mackenzie asked him.

"Honestly, you, Rachel, and the few times I saw Serena, y'all made it sound like fun. Also, my parents didn't want me hanging around the house on a Saturday night too when they could have justified kicking me out."

"You look amazing right now," Mackenzie complimented him.

"Thank you," he said. "You look lovely as well. Is that your sister's dress you mentioned?"

"It is! I'm surprised it fits me, but the other dress I had was stained the other day by my two siblings running around the house with paint."

"Oh no," Mike replied.

"It's okay. They finally got punished for their shenanigans, and I'm at the prom in a pretty dress," Mackenzie smirked.

"There's always an upside," Mike said.

"Indeed." Mackenzie smiled.

The song ended and the two broke off to their friends. The dance went as expected. Like Mike predicted, kids grinded in front of Sister Mary Beth, everyone crowded the floors for the line dancing, and Mackenzie found herself giving and receiving compliments from Leah Walters in the bathroom. Mackenzie ended the night dancing with Dave until Mike cut in.

"Just can't get enough of me?" Mackenzie asked.

"No, I'm doing this for the drama," Mike said. "Does this look like a movie? You know where the one guy cuts the other dude and the dancing couple has a serious conversation?"

"I don't think you're serious enough," Mackenzie said.

"Okay, well, then who do you think was to blame for World War One?" Mike asked.

"The Austrians, I guess?"

"Not the Germans? How logical of you! I will find out your secrets and the government's cover-up plot, Mackenzie Joan Bishop," Mike said.

Mackenzie took advantage of the spy thriller drama and leaned into his ear, "Whatever you try will fail, Michael Jeremy Sienkiewicz."

Mike's mouth opened as the song ended. Mackenzie still couldn't quite tell when his seriousness and silliness started and ended. As his mouth was agape, Dave invited him to get junk food with the group.

"Eh, why not," Mike said and followed the group.

As the girls gorged on milkshakes and Luke taught everyone how to properly dip French fries into ice cream, Mike stopped for a moment.

"You know, I guess prom is actually fun," he said.

"Duh," Serena chimed in. "We don't do these things for torture."

"I do fun things for torture; that's why I'm in AP Statistics," Mike replied.

"And why we're all in Catholic school," Mackenzie snarked.

"Almost free," Luke mumbled.

"We should all do this next year," Mike went on. "Dave will be a junior. Serena can invite you back, Luke. Next year? Next year? Next year," he said as he pointed to each individual in the group. Luke and Serena blushed while Dave and Mackenzie nodded along.

"Sure," Mackenzie smiled.

Chapter Thirty-Nine

Rachel returned from Maine a week later to a condolence card Mackenzie and Serena taped to her locker. She wasn't close with her grandma, so she didn't cry much at the funeral, but it was hard hearing how a healthy eighty seven-year-old just passed away in her sleep. The funeral went as well as expected. Her family arrived in Portland the previous Friday night, attended the funeral a week later, and stuck around to help with the will and collect items of Grandmother Clarice's possessions. Rachel took a few rings for her keepsake, and her mother took back some paintings.

It wasn't until she went back to school and stared at her locker for a second, she realized St. Joseph's went on without her. Teachers were giving her extra assignments from the days she missed along with notes to help. Everyone was also talking about prom. She saw Mackenzie and Serena's social media posts the other day but never quite registered that she missed prom. Before heading off to lunch, Mackenzie and Serena hugged her at her locker.

"How was the funeral?" Serena asked.

"It was okay. Nothing major happened. None of my uncles or aunts broke out fighting," Rachel said. "I didn't know my grandma super well though. She was nice in the last few years we visited..."

"I'm sorry, Rachel," Mackenzie said.

"Not your fault" she replied. "It's like I've forgotten all about school the last week or so. How was prom?"

Mackenzie started by saying she ended up taking Dave due to complications. She and Serena talked about going out to eat when they realized the subject of Mike showing up to the dance was going to be hard for Rachel. They both stared at each other for a few seconds.

"What?" Rachel asked. "What happened next?"

"Don't get upset, but then Mike showed up," Serena said.

"Oh, I thought he didn't like prom," Rachel replied.

"That's what we thought," Mackenzie said. "But he came dressed in a tux."

"With a purple bowtie, which I'd like to point out would have matched you, Mack, if you wore your other dress," Serena added. "I think he was trying to match you on purpose."

Serena realized what she was saying in front of Rachel and immediately stopped. Rachel, however, didn't seem to notice the comment at all. "So, what did you guys like about the prom?"

Mackenzie wanted to say Mike's surprise but was cautious.

"I liked just dancing to slow songs that weren't 'Can You Feel the Love Tonight' or 'Don't Want to Miss a Thing,'" Mackenzie said.

"Yeah, I liked just spinning in my dress with Luke," Serena added as she picked up on Mackenzie's word choice.

"Okay," Rachel said, still dazed from getting readjusted to school. As her friends walked away, it hit her. *Did Mike really go to prom?! I missed prom and Mike?* Rachel slammed her locker so hard it swung back open and almost hit her. Embarrassed, she closed it gently, but snapped her lock.

✱✱✱

After school that day, Mackenzie and Serena were hanging out at the latter's house to study for the AP Euro exam they were taking in a week. Sometime around getting bored talking about World War II, they decided to talk about the prom.

"So, let me get this straight, you told Mike you were wearing one of two dresses," Serena started. "Your date cancels on you at the last minute and then he swoops in dressed similar to you. He also asked you to dance at the end. Don't you think that's almost fishy?"

"Fishy?" Mackenzie began. "How so?"

"Do you ever think Mike likes you?" Serena said.

"A dance does not mean he likes me," Mackenzie said.

"Hear me out, let's expand it past the dance," Serena said. "He has invited you out to a weekly dinner where it's you guys and two dudes who are discerning the priesthood. No one else, just you. He also sits with you on band rides and trusts you with his middle name. When you went to Boston, he spent most of his time with you until people started asking if you were dating. Then prom happens. Mackenzie, I think he likes you."

"Stop it." Mackenzie dreaded the thought. "He's a great friend. Friends are like that. What's the difference if you and I did all that stuff?"

"Well, for one, we've intentionally stated that we're platonic friends. Another reason is that I don't casually flirt with you in class and at our lockers and spend time with you on long trips. He's spending time with you because he wants to be with you, and he's more open around you because he trusts you because he likes you. He's never shown any interest in anyone like this or tried the same tactics on anyone we know. You've been trying to know him since the beginning of sophomore year, and after he stopped pushing you out, he let you in. I mean, he even let you in after you tried to stop talking to him for a few weeks. He's interested in you."

"Oh hell." Mackenzie gave up. "I think you've finally pointed out something I've been trying to avoid. Mike likes me, and that makes me nervous."

Neither spoke as if a third person was listening in on them. Rachel spent a year and a half pursuing a guy who showed no interest in her, but he showed interest in her best friend.

"I can't do this to Rachel," Mackenzie fretted.

"Do you like Mike?" Serena asked.

"No, he's really just a good friend," Mackenzie insisted. "He could be another brother to me."

"Well, then what's there to worry about if you don't like him back?"

"Rachel will lose her mind. You know she gets super jealous. She'll think I betrayed her by making him like me. We also made that pact that the only thing that will ruin our friendship is if a guy came between us and one of us liked him but was better for the other."

"But wouldn't you be better for Mike? I mean, you're super close and all. You have his attention."

"But I don't like Mike, so what's the point of telling her? It would only make her mad," Mackenzie said. "She still thinks they're better together anyway. That's what she tells me all the time after they do stats homework together. Rachel joined a community band and learned trombone to be with him. She's making herself better suited for him. If she knew what's going on, she would lose it."

"How could she lose it? We're just in high school?" Serena asked. "Life moves on?"

"You've seen her get mad at little things, Serena," Mackenzie said. "Remember that time she injured classmates playing volleyball when she tried taking her anger out in P.E. class? She told me she was mad that Mary Kate Love got a better grade on an AP practice test than her. Next thing you know, Katie Birch has a black eye for a week. I don't want a black eye, Serena. I like my eyes. Do you want to get black eyes?"

"Why me? I'm not part of this," Serena asked.

"Serena, we both know she takes her anger out on you."

Serena thought about what her friend said for a minute before getting on board with the idea.

"Fine, we keep it a secret but only for everyone's good. She may be in denial about Mike not showing interest in her, but only Rachel can find out about Mike liking you from her own investigations."

The girls shook hands before getting back to studying. It wasn't a secret if three people knew it and Mackenzie hoped Rachel never found out.

Chapter Fourty

The next day, Rachel approached Mackenzie at her locker before Mike arrived.

"Hey," Rachel said quietly.

"Hey, Rachel, how are you?" Mackenzie asked as she grabbed her books for the next few classes.

"Can we talk?" Rachel asked.

Mackenzie's heart stopped for a second, thinking she knew Mike was interested in her.

"Yeah, okay."

"Did Mike dance with anyone at the prom?"

"Well, Dave had him dance with me for the second slow song and then he cut in between me and Dave during the last song because he wanted to reenact a movie cliche, but I don't think he danced with any other girls."

"Oh good." Rachel sighed. "I don't know what I was thinking. I just figured he might like someone else, but I trust you guys, and I trust that you're just friends."

"Well, that's all it is," Mackenzie said nervously as she walked off to her first class.

✳ ✳ ✳

Mackenzie found herself avoiding Rachel under the guise of studying for AP exams. It was going well leading into the exams until she had to take them and then not have a reason to avoid her friend. She had three weeks left of the school year before she could dodge Rachel with a summer job.

Since AP classes were done but there were a few weeks left in the year, most teachers filled their class periods with filler. During Sharpe's class, Mike and Mackenzie would snark at the black and white historical films he made them watch, and, in Miss Wilson's class, Mackenzie found herself zoning out to film versions of books they read. One day after excusing herself to go to the bathroom in Miss Wilson's class, she ran into Ron Hitchcock in the hall.

"Hey, how's it going?" she asked.

"It's good. It's fine," he said.

They stared at each other.

"So, listen, prom. Leah is just a friend. She asked me before you did, and I didn't want to say no to her," Ron said, looking down.

"Hey, it's okay," Mackenzie stopped him. "It's just prom."

"So anyway, is there any chance you're free Friday?"

"Yeah, I am," Mackenzie said.

"Want to go, like, see a movie?"

"Sure. Which one?"

"Maybe the new superhero one, unless you don't like those."

Mackenzie was surprised at Ron's forwardness. He was cute. And this would distance herself from the rather flirty Mike, so Rachel wouldn't have to worry.

"I was looking forward to Miss Apocalypse and the Heartbreak King!" she found herself saying excitedly.

"Okay, so I'll pick you up at six then," he asked. "Text me your address later."

"Sure!"

Later at lunch, Mackenzie found herself prepping for her first date.

"So, I think Ron asked me out," she told Rachel. "Not as boyfriend-girlfriend but he is taking me to a movie."

"I think that's a date." Rachel perked up. "I'm so happy for you! Do you think you'll date?"

"We'll see," Mackenzie said.

"If you guys date, maybe I can get the guts to ask out Mike and we can double date," Rachel added.

"Do you think you'll really ask him?"

"I mean, if you can date Ron, then I probably have a shot with Mike."

Mackenzie held herself back from saying she might have to wait an eternity for Rachel to ask out Mike.

Chapter Fourty-One

On Friday, Ron arrived promptly at six while Mackenzie was still getting ready. She wasn't quite sure what to wear, so she threw on a clean pair of jeans and a plain purple t-shirt. Ron took her to a Mexican restaurant near the theatre.

As Ron grabbed a tortilla chip, he asked, "You heard about the cheese dip here? It's queso good."

Mackenzie chuckled. "That's so cheesy it could be part of the dip."

Ron smiled.

"So, what do you think will happen in the movie?" Mackenzie asked to fill the silence.

"I think the Heartbreak King will die. It's time for Eli Wilson to leave the franchise," Ron said.

"I don't know; these superhero characters never stay dead," Mackenzie said.

"Maybe, but it would be nice if they let a character stay dead for once," Ron said. "Do you want to go over to the pharmacy and buy dollar candy to sneak in beforehand?"

"What do you think I brought this big purse for?" Mackenzie said as she held up her tote bag.

The two teenagers watched the movie, feeling awkward. Mackenzie left her hand out for Ron to hold, but he seemed to keep his either in his pockets or with his bag of sour worms. She gave up worrying about halfway through the movie and began snickering with Ron during certain moments.

"I feel like Atlas just sits there and never does anything and we're expected to believe he's a threat," Mackenzie whispered.

"A threat to his health for sitting so long," Ron said.

After the movie ended, Ron and Mackenzie patiently waited for the post-credits screen to roll.

"He's dead," Ron said.

"Totally not dead," Mackenzie argued.

The Heartbreak King was lying on the floor, bleeding out of his chest when he got back up, healed his wound with magic, and called and asked his sidekick what was the German word for revenge.

"I KNEW IT," Mackenzie cheered.

"Congrats on guessing what everyone knew," Ron snarked.

After the movie was over, Ron drove Mackenzie home. Then they stood talking on her porch for fifteen minutes.

"So, I had fun," Mackenzie said.

"Me too," he replied.

"You're a great guy. I wish I knew you better," Mackenzie started. She didn't notice Ron leaning in. "It was really—" She was cut off by Ron's lips on hers.

Mackenzie didn't know what she was doing or why her eyes were open during it, so she held onto his arms and tried to keep it going with her eyes shut. After fifteen seconds, Ron leaned back and opened his eyes.

"So, I'll talk to you later," Ron said, blushing as he walked to his car.

"Yeah, you know how," Mackenzie said as her face turned red.

Mackenzie stood on her porch as she watched him drive away.

"That was nice," Mackenzie heard herself say out loud as she reached for the front door's knob.

Chapter Fourty-Two

That Monday, students handed out yearbooks to sign and cleaned out their lockers. Mackenzie, Rachel, and Serena were talking by the first's locker as mutual friends approached them and they all went around swapping yearbooks.

"If anyone writes 'H.A.G.S.' in my yearbook one more time, I'm going to groan all the way until we graduate next year," Rachel said while getting her book back from Kate Parsons.

"Um, sorry," Kate said as she took her book back from Serena.

Rachel began to groan but was interrupted by Ron Hitchcock.

"Hey, Mackenzie, can I sign your yearbook?"

"Sure, someone around here has it," she said as she pulled out random assignment papers she didn't need anymore. Catie Arnold handed Mackenzie's yearbook she was previously writing in to Ron. As he began to sign it, he started talking to Mackenzie.

"So, what are you doing this summer?" he asked.

"I'm working at my parent's business again," Rachel interrupted.

Ron ignored her.

"I'm working at the day camp at the local gym. You?" she asked, blushing as she turned to face him.

"No way, me too!" he blushed back and attempted to hold his hand up for a high five. "So, um, I had a fun time Friday. Would you want to do it again this Friday?"

"We have our sleepover this Friday," Rachel turned to Mackenzie.

"Yeah, I can see you again!" Mackenzie said loudly. "What time?"

"Maybe six again?" Ron offered. "We could go mini-golfing."

"I would love that," Mackenzie said.

"Cool." He handed back her yearbook. "I'll see you later."

Serena made sure Ron was out of earshot before asking Mackenzie about her previous date.

"That's awesome, Mackenzie," Serena said. "How was your first date with him anyways?"

"It was good! We had a lot of fun, and he's partial to dad puns, which I appreciate." Mackenzie smiled.

"That's cool, but you're blowing off our annual start of summer sleepover?" Rachel asked harshly. "We were planning on having it Friday after we all got out from finals."

"We can move it to Saturday," Serena corrected her.

"I guess we could." Rachel sighed. "I hate it when plans change."

"But this is good for Mackenzie!" Serena said brightly.

"True," Rachel said. "We can plan on her telling us about their great date."

"Who's great date?" Mike interrupted as he got to his locker.

"Oh, I have a second date, nothing big, with Ron on Friday," Mackenzie dismissed.

"Oooh, Ron Hitchcock or Ron Wilkerson?" Mike asked. "Because Ron Hitchcock is a hottie, but Wilkerson has seen Ghostbusters 500 times."

"Hitchcock," Rachel said seriously. "Can I sign your yearbook?"

"Sure," Mike said as he gave it to her. As he opened his locker, a pile of papers, writing utensils, and some textbooks spilled onto the floor.

"Oh my gosh, we can't take you anywhere, can we?" Mackenzie joked.

"Nah, I'm a disappointment to all," Mike joked.

"You're not a disappointment!" Rachel fussed as she bent down to help Mike with his mess. "You're great at being messy. What are you doing for summer again?"

"I'm back in Jersey with the boys. We're going to try P90X every day and get bulked up to action star size," Mike said. "What are you guys doing?"

"Back at my parents' business," Rachel said. "Hopefully not making as many coffee runs as I did last year."

"I'll still be scooping ice cream for minimum wage," Serena said.

"And I'll start at a gym's summer camp this year," Mackenzie added, taking his yearbook from Rachel when she remembered she already scribbled a note there and gave it back to him.

"And you'll be smooching Hitchcock too," Mike added. Mackenzie blushed even more.

The last thing she took out of her locker was the picture of her, Rachel, and Serena posing outside the bowling alley. *Times flies*, she thought.

✷ ✷ ✷

That Friday, after finals let out, Mackenzie was ready for the next chapter of her life. She was ready for a potential summer romance, video chats from Mike, and sleepovers with her girls all before her last year of high school. She got ready on time when Ron rang her family's front doorbell that night. He took her out for mini-golf where they both took ten tries at each hole.

"You know, for being an athlete, I'm pretty terrible at golf," Ron joked.

"I'm just happy there's no one waiting behind us," Mackenzie said.

Ron kissed her for the second time by the course's windmill. This kiss was much less awkward than the first one. After finishing all eighteen holes, the two sat down for ice cream.

"So, what's the deal with you and Mike?" Ron asked.

Mackenzie rolled her eyes.

"We're just friends, trust me. He's more like an annoying brother than anything."

"Okay, so I shouldn't be worried?"

"Why would you be worried?"

"Because, Mackenzie Bishop, you are sweet and funny and smart and beautiful. Will you be my girlfriend?" he said, blushing.

"Yeah of course!" Mackenzie said.

She was excited to have her first boyfriend ever. He was cute, charming, and gave her the time of day.

Ron kissed her a second time that night. For Mackenzie, everything about the moment was perfect.

"So, like I know it's our senior year, but what do you want to do after graduation?" he asked.

"I'm applying for a few music programs. The University of Chicago is my reach school since the acceptance rate there is tiny. But I also like UVA and Loyola for college."

"Okay, that would be far if you went to Illinois. I'm just looking at in-state schools," Ron said as he held her hand.

"Well, we're a long way from worrying about this," Mackenzie said. "Let's just focus on tonight."

"Yeah, I just worry about things easily," Ron said with his head down.

"It's good to live a little in the moment," Mackenzie said. "Tomorrow's not guaranteed."

Ron nodded before they kissed again.

Chapter Fourty-Three

That summer went as smoothly as Mackenzie and Ron's third kiss. Mackenzie learned how to be in a relationship and spent most of her nights talking to Ron or occasionally chatting with Mike. She also got into recording artist and alternative musician Kevin Scarpino and bought tickets to see him in October with Ron, who was along for the ride. Whatever she was into, he would take interest in and nodded happily when she said she got nosebleed seats.

As band camp drew near, she felt a sense of dread about getting back to the grind. Mrs. King personally emailed her that she wanted to see her on the first day of practice without further explanation. As Mackenzie drove up to the first day of practice, she kept thinking, *Don't panic.* As she walked up to the field, she heard Mrs. King yelling out at her to join Fae Edmondson, Katie Sims, Tim Sherman, Lizzie Moon, and John Murphy from separate sections to meet her.

"As all of you know, you're in your senior year," Mrs. King began. "All of you have shown leadership qualities over the years since you began, so I am making each of you your section's leaders."

Mackenzie couldn't say a word; she was so happy. After the meeting about expectations and how to handle band camp as the official leaders, the seniors broke off to their separate sections.

"Hey, stranger, what happened to you?" Mike said to her.

"Hey, it's Section Leader Stranger to you," Mackenzie said gleefully.

"No way," Mike said before high fiving her. His hand hit a little harder than it used to. Mackenzie took him in and realized he gained five pounds of muscles from the last time she saw him.

"You really took that summer challenge seriously," she said.

"You have no idea," Mike said. "I'm going to have to order salads at Dave Dinners now. My friends and I also made a bet about being the most fit by graduation."

"That's really intense, but I'm proud of you," Mackenzie said.

"Thanks," Mike said. "I'm proud of you getting section leader."

"Thanks."

Mackenzie looked at her wristwatch to see it was time to start band camp for her section.

"Bones! Gather it in!" she yelled loudly. She saw her friends and a plethora of new faces show up. "Welcome, back. I am Mackenzie Bishop to those who don't know me and Section Leader Mackenzie Bishop to Mike here. We are going to have fun and behave ourselves so we don't run hills for the next three weeks. Are we clear?"

All the new kids awkwardly nodded while the returners laughed.

"Now we will all go around saying our names, grades, and the weirdest incident you got into with your trombone. You know my name, I'm a senior, and one time I got my finger caught in a key during halftime."

Everyone laughed as she passed the ice breaker to Dave.

Mackenzie was still on her summer peak and not worried about crashing down into the school year. When she went home, she looked at her phone to see missed texts from Ron and messages from friends asking to compare schedules. Ready or not, Mackenzie was going to start her senior year on top.

Chapter Fourty-Four

Mackenzie strode into St. Joseph's hallways the first day of classes, ready for the year. She saw her friends approach her as she held Ron's hand.

"Hey!" Rachel squealed as she hugged her friend. She stared at Ron for a second. "Hey, Ron, welcome back."

"Hey, Rachel, how was your summer?" he asked.

"It was good! What are you up to?" Rachel asked.

"I'm just walking her to her first class before I go to Pre-Calc," he said.

"Okay, see you later," Rachel said, annoyed as she passed them in the halls.

"Okay. What's wrong already?" Serena asked as they headed to the choir room.

"Shouldn't she be hanging out with us first?"

"She's dating Ron, Rachel. He comes first now. Shouldn't you be happy for her?"

"I am, but I feel like we're losing her attention already."

"It's day one of school. We haven't even had a single class yet. We have plenty of time to hang out with Mack. What would happen if you dated Mike and acted like that to Mackenzie and me?"

"Well, for one thing, he's everyone's friend, so we would hang out longer with everyone," Rachel hissed. "I just feel like we don't have much time left together before college. I just don't want to waste it."

"Let's ask them to sit with us at lunch," Serena said.

"If we get lunch with her," Rachel grumbled.

Rachel was right. She didn't get lunch with Mackenzie, Mike, or Serena. None of her close friends had lunch with her because she was stuck with the average kids taking Mr. John Ford's Christian Vocations class instead of whatever classes they had.

Rachel was already feeling bad about the first day back, and her lunch situation didn't make it any better. She went to the girls' bathroom to have a private moment. She stared at her reflection wondering why she got so jealous in the first place. She was a little upset because Mackenzie found a boyfriend before she got together with Mike. That one stung. But it also hurt too to see that fact now everywhere she went with Mackenzie. Her friend would end up texting Ron during their sleepovers and wasn't able to hang out as much with her during the summer because she was with him. She imagined she couldn't have girl-to-girl conversations with Mackenzie anymore at school because Ron was going to always be there. Because of that, she felt like her friendship was being wasted. No one would give her the time of day because they were busy. Mackenzie had a boy toy, Mike was elusive, and she just didn't feel like hanging out with Serena because the two were starting to clash more and more these days. It didn't help that when Rachel was trying to fantasize about something, Serena's blunt words would cut through them.

Rachel knew she had issues, but she was trying to work on her jealousy on her own. She knew she could be judgmental. So, was she being overly harsh on Mackenzie for dating Ron Hitchcock? Possibly. Would she have to face it head-on? Maybe not. She could always focus on getting with Mike, no matter how fruitless it seemed.

After school that day, Rachel was feeling more out of it. Her locker was on the school's top floor, while Mackenzie, Mike, and Serena's lockers were on the bottom. Serena and Mackenzie had the same locker block while Mike was down the hall from them. When Rachel went to find her friends, it wasn't hard spotting Mackenzie considering she and Ron were making out in front of her locker.

"Hi," Rachel said, annoyed.

The couple broke from their embrace.

"Hey, Rachel, how is it going?" Mackenzie said obliviously.

"It's fine," she lied. "How are your classes?"

"Good! Ron and I don't have a class together though. Mike, Serena, and I have AP English Literature and AP Gov though! Also, Mike is in Art I with me."

"Forget about Mike; we're here now," Ron said before going for another smooch.

Rachel squinted in anger before walking away. She noticed Serena was still there before heading off to field hockey practice.

"Did you hear that?" Rachel whispered to Serena.

Serena rolled her eyes as she closed her locker.

"Just be glad you don't have lunch with them. I'm surprised the teachers there didn't pull them off each other."

✗ ✗ ✗

The next day at school wasn't much of a change, but Rachel was happy she had AP Calculus with Mike. She walked quickly to get the empty seat next to his.

"Hi, Mike," she squeaked.

"Ready to die again?" he asked.

"Always." Rachel smiled. "Are you doing community band again?"

"No, I'm too busy with AP classes, college applications, and marching band."

"Oh," she said, realizing she'd be alone this term every Monday night.

Rachel found solace in that the two of them had AP Physics together after calc.

Luck was against Rachel for Y days because she still had lunch alone. Mike was off to band while Rachel was in Bioethics again. The end of the day brought much of the same. Mackenzie and Ron were still kissing at her locker while she and Serena rolled their eyes.

"Maybe this will stop soon since they'll see each other every day," Serena suggested.

Chapter Fourty-Five

Serena was wrong. Mackenzie and Ron were stuck together like flies in a honey trap. It seemed like the teachers were never looking their way when the pair made out in the halls. After class, practice, and even football games, the two were constantly seen together. Even Serena was a little tired of seeing Ron hanging on to Mackenzie like a cape. It was finally one Friday night when St. Joseph's football had a bye week the girls finally held a sleepover for the first time that semester. Mackenzie brought up how close she felt to Ron.

"I really like him, but he always needs attention," Mackenzie said. "It's like he can't go five minutes without me, but I also need a break to take a breath and, you know, focus on myself."

"That's tough. Have you told him that?" Serena asked.

"Yeah, but he still clings on tightly," Mackenzie said.

"Why don't you break up with him?" Rachel said suddenly, looking up from painting her nails.

The other girls stared at her.

"No! He's great. He's just a high school boy," Mackenzie said as her phone buzzed to another of Ron's texts. "He'll come around to what I'm saying soon."

✻ ✻ ✻

Mackenzie was wrong. Ron was clingy as ever and now seemed to make a point to text or call her every time she was away from him. Mackenzie would start to tell him she needed a few minutes away from him, but it would make him scared she was breaking up with him. So, then she would need to reassure him for ten minutes she wasn't leaving and then he would cling to her for the rest of the day. Mackenzie started finding class time more relaxing than being with Ron.

"But I want to see you this weekend, Mackenzie. Your face is so beautiful," Ron would whine in the hallways.

"My grandpa turns one hundred this weekend. We've gone over this; I'll be in another state," Mackenzie said, annoyed.

It all came to a boiling point at Michelle's eighteenth birthday party. Her old friend reconnected with her, Rachel, and Serena that summer and they tried their best to hang out with her when they weren't busy with school or extracurriculars. Anytime Michelle met Mackenzie, Ron tagged along. Mackenzie was glad he didn't join for her birthday party.

Mackenzie, Rachel, and Serena were happy to attend Michelle's birthday party even though they didn't know her friends from public school. Michelle planned to order stuff from infomercials and buy lottery tickets to celebrate being a legal adult. Right before Michelle blew out her birthday candles, Mackenzie felt her phone go off. She knew it was Ron and ignored it by turning off her ringer. After opening a few presents, Mackenzie was ready to order some silly stuff they found during commercials. Mackenzie felt her phone buzz again. She picked it up and left the room.

"Hey," she said.

Everyone could hear the one side of Mackenzie's phone call.

"No, I'm at Michelle's. I've told you this."

"They'll be all right," Rachel said, trying to divert attention.

Rachel was wrong.

"No, you're not being sweet; you're being clingy," Mackenzie raised her voice.

Everyone overheard her.

"It's not cute. Also, you know what's not cute? How you have to flex in front of every guy we know that you're somehow the star quarterback. You aren't even being recruited for colleges!"

Everyone sat silent.

"And I like kissing, but isn't it a little weird we have to kiss every time we're in front of my friends?... No, that's just weird."

None of her friends were making eye contact in the other room. Serena fiddled with her fingernails while Rachel observed her class ring.

"No, I have the right to spend time with my friends and my family and not have you be my freaking shadow everywhere I go. Stop calling me, stop texting me, stop constantly telling me you love me, and get out of my life! It's over!"

Mackenzie went to the bathroom to wash her face while everyone else at the party started calling the 1-800 number for a knife set being advertised on the television.

"What a dick," Rachel heard Mackenzie mumble as they all went to the local gas station for a lottery ticket.

Rachel was not surprised when she woke up to a group text from Mackenzie saying she and Ron broke up the night before.

Chapter Fourty-Six

The break up was hard for Mackenzie, but not because she was sad about Ron. She was relieved she didn't have to have her phone on her constantly or make sure she wasn't speaking about Mike around other guys. She went back to Dave Dinners now that Ron wasn't there to take her home after practice.

However, Ron went around the school telling everyone she cheated on him with a community college student. Her friends believed her, and her section stood by her, but some members of the football team and their girlfriends would give her dirty looks in the halls. Being the star senior quarterback now, Ron had a few fangirls at the school who weren't afraid to spread rumors that Mackenzie was a slut.

Mackenzie did her best to avoid them, but it was hard seeing classmates she was friendly with turn their backs on her. After venting about her recent freedom to her friends at dinner, Kevin and Dave felt the need to speak up.

"Well, he was clearly showing red flags, but we're glad you're through with it," Kevin said.

"Yeah, we were concerned for a bit but didn't know how to help you, so we just decided to add you to our prayers," Dave said.

"Thanks, guys, I appreciate it," Mackenzie said.

Mike stayed quiet throughout dinner as everyone else talked. After finishing his salad, he walked Mackenzie to her car.

"I'm sorry the breakup is so troubling," Mike said. "You don't deserve any of this ire from classmates."

"Thanks. I know you have been defending me to classmates," Mackenzie said. "The guys aren't as much trouble as the females at our school; I get the nastiest looks."

"Just keep your head up. Their necks are going to hurt from looking down on you so much," Mike said.

"Hey," Mackenzie said. "I was going to see Kevin Scarpino in concert in a few weeks with Ron, but since we're over, do you want his ticket?"

"Yeah! He's that jazz musician, right?" Mike snarked. "I may have to leave early to take my Alzheimer's medication."

"I'll get you back before bedtime that Saturday night," Mackenzie joked.

He hugged her before driving away. Mackenzie went back home and worked on her AP Government assignments while texting Mike and Serena about the class. She was going to be fine, but she knew she'd have to go through hell until Christmas before other students lost interest in her.

She texted Rachel about the concert tickets to give her a heads up so she wouldn't lash out in anger or jealousy. Rachel texted back that she was unbothered.

Mackenzie kept her head up until the football game that Friday. She was walking back to the band room when she heard a few cheerleaders whisper "slut" as she went by. Cheer captain Leah Walters openly walked up to her and said, "So since you're now free, who's next on your list to destroy?"

"Yeah, Mackenzie, what man at the school are you going to ruin next, a soccer player or member of our class's top five percentile?" fellow cheerleader Mary Andrews joined in.

"No one," Mike suddenly interrupted. "She's not a man-eater. She wouldn't go for those types anyway because she's too good for them. So, either find her a Pulitzer Prize winner or move along before I report your bullying to Vice Principal Nelson, who's twenty feet ahead of us."

The two cheerleaders scowled and walked away. Mackenzie stood frozen in place. She wasn't sure what just happened, but her eyes were full of tears. She hugged Mike for what felt like eons.

"I think you need a calm night at home alone," Mike said as he walked her to her car. They talked casually for a few minutes as Rachel and Serena approached them.

"Ready for the party?" Rachel asked.

"Eh, I think I'm going to turn in early. I'm tired," Mackenzie said with her voice croaking.

"Okay, have a good night," Rachel said. "Mike, are you still ready to party?"

"No, I think I'm tired too, but thanks," he said before getting to his car.

Rachel and Serena left, and Mike watched Mackenzie drive away. Mackenzie read Mike's "talk to me if you need me" text when she got home.

Mackenzie felt tears coming up. She wasn't crying from the harassment she experienced but because she felt full-hearted from his text. She felt what he did was too good for her. Mackenzie wanted to spend all the coming hours with Mike, talking to him and laughing with him, and wished she gave him time this summer instead of Ron. She wanted to be in Mike's arms.

Chapter Fourty-Seven

Mackenzie woke up with the same emotions she had last night, wanting Mike in her presence. She was also confused by her feelings and decided to explore them. Mackenzie knew Mike was always there for her. From being sophomores snickering in Miss Wilson's Honors English class and when he invited her to the band party, the times he took her to Dave Dinners, and how he arrived at prom matching her. Everything he did lead up to this.

Mackenzie knew he liked her and thought dating Ron would end any confusing thoughts or feelings she had. But dating Ron and ending it with him made her realize she truly liked Mike. He put her happiness above others, he was patient, and he was a fun guy. Mike stood by her even when she almost revealed his dumb secret.

The Boston trip was still on her mind, and she thought back to a few weeks earlier when Mike texted her that he was still applying to Harvard and told her to continue her application. It was sweet he paid for her application fee when she maybe spent twenty dollars on him at the school's bookstore.

Mackenzie saw her friend grow more and more attractive every year. *He also has a nice butt,* she thought as a smile grew on her face. But also, his eyes were deep blue, and she was ready to stare into them for longer when she pictured him in her head.

Damn, Mackenzie thought. *I like Mike. And so much more than that crush from two years ago.*

She texted Serena there was an emergency and to come over immediately. Ten minutes later, Serena was out of breath outside Mackenzie's house. She nearly ran over her friend when the latter opened the door.

"ARE YOU OKAY? DO WE NEED TO CALL 911?" Serena panicked.

"Calm down, Serena!" Mackenzie said. "Just get in my house."

Serena joined Mackenzie inside the Bishop residence and noticed that as disorderly as the house was, nothing was off. They walked to Mackenzie's room and the latter shut her door.

"So, the emergency is this and it's kind of a long story, but last night some cheerleaders started calling me a slut and asking who I was going to date and destroy next," Mackenzie started.

"Those jerks!" Serena said.

"Hold on," Mackenzie continued. "Mike came to my aid and defended me. He calmed me down and walked me to my car."

"That's sweet," Serena said.

"And when I got home last night, I realized something. I just wanted to be with Mike. I think I have feelings for him, and I think they've been here since maybe spring. I just kept denying them and went out with Ron to ignore them."

"Oh my gosh," Serena said. "What are you gonna do?"

"That's the problem," Mackenzie said, "I don't know. Rachel likes him, and I don't think she'll just give up on someone she's been pursuing for like two and half years."

"But if he likes you too and asks you out then what are you going to do?"

"Date him because he thinks we're better together, I suppose." Mackenzie sighed. "And hope Rachel doesn't get outright mad at me."

"Maybe there's another option?" Serena asked. "Can't you be direct with Rachel? No, I just heard that out loud. She wouldn't like it. She would kill you."

"So, I guess that's all we got," Mackenzie said.

"Well, let's hope this works out," Serena said. "I'm so happy for you. You guys would make a great couple."

After Serena left that day, Mackenzie and Mike texted back and forth about the night before, homework, rock and roll, and band.

Mackenzie belly laughed for a good five minutes when she read "#Istandwithmackenziebishop" sent from Mike.

***

That Monday, Mackenzie realized she would have to avoid Rachel for a while so she wouldn't raise suspicion. When she made it to AP Government, she sat anxiously between Serena and Mike.

"How's it going, Mackenzie?" he asked.

"All right," she replied. Mackenzie noticed out of the corner of her eye that Serena was ignoring them. Throughout the class, Serena wouldn't make her usual snarky faces at either of them or try signing to them when Mr. Addison said something weird or showed political biases. She genuinely paid attention to Mr. Addison's lecture in that class. After class ended, Serena stood up quickly, gave a "see you later" to her friends, and ran out. It then clicked with Mackenzie that her friend was trying to give them space.

"I think our daughter behaved herself for the first time today," Mike joked to Mackenzie as they left the classroom.

"Our daughter?" Mackenzie asked, surprised.

"Well, Serena is the baby of this group, and I feel like we cover for her when Addison catches her doing faces or signing," Mike said.

"All right, but when did we get married?" Mackenzie joked back.

"We're living in sin, Mackenzie," he replied as he picked up his books.

Mackenzie blushed as they walked in different directions.

Mackenzie felt better coming to terms with her feelings. However, it hurt not being in a relationship with Mike every time they had class, lunch, band, and even Dave Dinner. They were such great friends and could transition to a couple easily, but there seemed to be a large gap between that transition.

✱ ✱ ✱

Two weeks after Mackenzie realized her feelings, Serena was sitting with her in her bedroom working on their AP Government homework.

"I just really want to see Mike," Mackenzie said.

"Why not?" Serena asked.

"I can't see him; it's a weeknight," she replied. "I feel crazy, like I'm going nuts without him here."

"You're not crazy; you have a crush," Serena replied. "You're a high school senior with a car and a cellphone. He's probably free right now."

"But what about you here?" she asked.

"This project isn't due until next Thursday. We have time."

"I have to see him," Mackenzie repeated. "I need to see him."

"Well then go!" Serena cheered.

"Okay, I'll be right back."

Mackenzie left her room without thinking, running out the front door without a coat.

What was normally a half-hour walk to Mike's house through the woods became an eighteen-minute sprint for Mackenzie. The walk she could normally take to his house in the woods was easy to find during the day, but even in the darkness, she felt her way through the woods on pure adrenaline. She texted him on the way there that she needed to see him. Mike was confused, but when she got outside his house, she saw his light on and his shadow leave his room. Waiting for him to come down took eons for her. He stood in his front door, confused at her sudden appearance.

"Mackenzie, what's up?" Mike said. "Where's your jacket? Why are you pacing quickly?"

"We should probably sit for this," she said anxiously as she found the wooden bench his parents had in their front yard. "This isn't easy to say."

"You can tell me anything," he said as he sat down next to her.

"I think I love you."

Chapter Fourty-Eight

Mike was quiet for a few minutes as Mackenzie could hear her heartbeat out of her chest. The crickets were chirping, and she was able to make out a few constellations in the sky while waiting for him to respond.

"Can you give me some time to think about this?" Mike asked.

"Sure," Mackenzie said as she felt her heart drop.

"You kind of just sprung it on me," Mike said. "I don't know how to feel."

"Okay," Mackenzie said.

"But I'll see you tomorrow," Mike added.

"Yeah," Mackenzie replied as she got up and started walking away.

Mackenzie went through the same woods and walked back to her house. As she walked, she picked up her phone and called Serena as adrenaline ran through her. After four rings, Serena's phone went to voicemail. Weird. Five minutes later, she got a call from Rachel.

"Mackenzie, are you okay?" Rachel asked.

"Yeah, why?"

"Serena's step-foster-whatever sister was at her house and saw you call her phone as it charged. Where are you?"

"I was just out for a walk," Mackenzie said.

She didn't want to mention Mike after this whole night.

"What were you guys doing together and where is she?" Rachel started inquiring.

"We were studying for AP Gov. She probably just forgot her phone at her house before she came over, but we finished half an hour ago, so she's probably still ignoring it."

Rachel accepted that answer before hanging up. After another twenty minutes, Mackenzie got home and was surprised Serena was still there and talking to her mother.

"Serena, you're still here? We finished homework half an hour ago," she said, surprised.

Serena looked unamused. "I know."

"But since you're here, I'm going to take you back to my room to finish one question," she said in front of her mom.

As they got to Mackenzie's room, both girls got more and more excited.

"What happened?" Serena asked.

"Well, I ended up running to his house and when he got out, I told him I loved him."

"What? You feel that seriously about him?"

"I don't know. I just blurted it out."

"What did he say?"

"He just told me to give him time."

"Weird," Serena said. "Are you okay?"

"I think I am," Mackenzie said. "Yeah, also I tried calling you, but your phone is at your house. For some reason, your cousin was there and saw it go off and told Rachel. So, she called me while going back."

"Yikes," Serena said. "Jess is here for a work trip. She knew I was studying but probably saw my phone and was worried anyways. So, what about Rachel?"

"We can't tell her about tonight," Mackenzie said. "I just told her I was going for a walk and you were supposed to be home. By the way, why are you still here?"

"After you ran out the door, I was about to leave, but Junie saw me and then talked my ear off about fourth grade. She then showed me her drawings and made me play dolls. Thankfully, your mom stopped her and then started talking my ear off. Apparently, you and I are both applying to Georgia State."

Mackenzie stopped for a moment to think. She wasn't applying to Georgia State but Georgia Southern. Mackenzie was so confused at the whole moment. She was just chasing Mike, got semi-rejected, was forced to talk to Rachel, and now was back to applying for colleges.

"I just can't believe I told him I loved him," Mackenzie said, sitting down.

"I know. I'm surprised too," Serena said as she hugged Mackenzie.

"But at the same time, I meant it," Mackenzie said.

"I'm so proud of you. That takes a lot of courage."

"Thanks. Note to self, on September 24, I told Mike I loved him"

Serena hugged her again before she headed home. She hoped her friend would be fine after all that happened in the span of two hours.

Mackenzie was not fine as she lay in bed that night crying. If Mike needed time, then he probably didn't like her in the first place. He was just being friendly this whole time... which was weird. He didn't like her but was still there for her as a friend, which didn't make much sense. Why would he coordinate and dance with her at the prom, save her in front of cheerleaders, and ask her to dinner with two possible seminarians if he didn't like her?

As she cried to sleep, she felt a little shunned. Tomorrow was going to be rough.

✱ ✱ ✱

The next day, Mackenzie woke up feeling empty. She didn't want to go to school, so she ran the family thermometer under hot water from the sink. Her busy parents bought it and let her stay home.

That day in class, Serena sat alone in AP Government, worried about her friend. Mike asked her about Mackenzie. She was kind of upset at him too, so she decided to sign to him that Mackenzie was sick with the zombie flu. Mike signed back at her that he didn't know the illness was real. Taken aback that Mike was finally good at ASL, she asked him when he learned.

"Since you were doing it, I figured I'd try to get fluent too," he signed.

Before she could sign back, Mr. Addison also signed to them, "Keep signing and it's lunch detention. Stop and I'll give you mercy detention."

Serena signed "sorry," and Mike sent "idiot," putting his fist to his forehead by mistake, to Mr. Addison. Mike was promptly given a lunch detention slip. That day at lunch, Serena decided to go with Mike to lunch detention.

"So, what's your deal, Mike?" Serena asked him.

"What?" Mike replied.

"Why are you so friendly to girls but don't date them when they show enough interest in you?" she inquired. "Are you using my friends for favors? Showing off to the other douches at this school? Covering up being gay?"

"No, I'm straight," Mike said. "But I like having girls who are friends. What's this about specifically?"

"Never mind," Serena mumbled, opening her lunchbox.

"I'm genuinely confused," Mike said. "Does this have to do with Mackenzie being out today? Also, why are you here? Addison didn't give you lunch detention."

"No, she wasn't feeling too well last night when she decided to take a walk at night. Hopefully, nothing was keeping her out long. Also, who said Addison is the reason I'm in lunch detention today?"

Mike was unsure if she knew about what happened the night before and decided to ignore her. Serena and Mike sat there awkwardly as they ate the rest of their lunch in silence with other students.

After school, Serena was approached by Rachel, which was a personal first in a few weeks.

"Hey," Rachel said calmly. "Are you okay?"

"Yeah, why not?" Serena asked.

"Oh, you just seem off today. I heard you got detention with Mike," Rachel replied.

"Yeah, that happened; he's still relearning ASL," Serena sighed. "But also Mr. Ford thought my skirt was too short."

"So, what happened to Mackenzie?"

"What do you mean?"

"Well, Mackenzie doesn't take many sick days, and this is the first time in a while. I talked to her last night, but she sounded fine to me."

"Maybe she wasn't as good as she sounded."

"Or maybe she's hiding something."

Serena hesitated.

"Rachel, we're all friends. Why would Mackenzie try to hide something? She probably just got sick and threw up and her parents finally paid attention to her and told her to take today off. You'll see her tomorrow."

"That's true, but also why have you guys been avoiding me for the last few weeks?"

Serena rolled her eyes. "We're not avoiding you; we've been busy with school and college applications. Also, I always have to approach you if you want to hang out with me. It's never the other way. You're being dramatic."

"Well maybe I just think you're busy and our interests are different," Rachel said. "Also, I am not dramatic!"

She huffed as she walked away.

Serena rolled her eyes as Rachel stormed off. She looked back into her locker and saw the photo of them and Mackenzie outside the bowling alley. *What the hell happened to cause this divide?* she thought.

Chapter Fourty-Nine

Mackenzie showed up at school the next day with bags under her eyes, her hair barely brushed, and almost unable to speak. Mike's silence was killing her.

"It's going to be okay." Serena hugged her at their lockers.

Mackenzie thought otherwise and actively told herself she was not going to be okay and was going to have to be okay with that. Mackenzie couldn't eat anything at lunch because she wasn't feeling hungry. She sat away from Mike in band class and after school practice. Neither was approaching the other. Neither showed up for Dave Dinner that week.

"Does this feel weird?" Dave asked Kevin as they sat across from each other.

"Totally," Kevin replied. "Mackenzie seems tired, but I don't know why Mike said no to tonight. He just said he wasn't coming."

"Maybe it's college application stress for the both of them," Dave said before taking a bite of his chili and pineapple hotdog.

College applications seemed to change all of the seniors' moods. Mackenzie still applied for the University of Chicago even though her chances of getting in there or Harvard were the same as time traveling to see dinosaurs. She was at least happy to have an outlet to type her feelings into her application essays. She was surprised that her parents let her apply to so many schools. She added Georgia Southern and Agnes Scott College, a small all-women liberal arts school, to her list. The latter had a good art program and because it was private, could offer more scholarships to her. She figured why not apply.

As she was answering minor questions on the Common App, she got a text from Mike.

Mike: Have you applied to Harvard yet?

Mackenzie: Just sent it last night. You?

Mike: I think I might rescind my application

Mackenzie: Hey, we made a pact. I apply, you apply. No take-backs

Mike: True

Mackenzie: I know where you live. Don't make me come over there and send it for you

Mike: Want to know the truth?

Mackenzie's heart skipped a bit.

Mackenzie: What?

Mike: I applied two months ago for early decision. I'll get my rejection letter around Christmas

Mackenzie: Be kind to yourself!

You'll get waitlisted at Christmas and rejected in the spring

Mackenzie and Mike found it easier to communicate after that exchange. As they got back to texting, they got back to talking to each other in class, the halls, and back at Dave Dinner after two weeks of leaving Kevin and Dave by themselves. It was two days before the Kevin Scarpino concert when Mike pulled Mackenzie aside after band practice.

"Hey, I know I've been leaving you on ice for the last three weeks and I'm sorry," Mike began, "but I need you to know that I really only see you as a friend. You're someone I trust and like to talk to, but I don't see us romantically and I need you to know that before we go to the concert so you don't think it's a date."

Mackenzie couldn't look Mike in the eyes. She knew she would break out crying if she did. Instead, she faced the freshmen trombones messing around across from her.

"Thanks for telling me," Mackenzie said. "I mean, I figured you probably didn't reciprocate feelings after not telling me for three weeks. But I appreciate it, and I wasn't thinking Saturday was a date. You were always going as my friend, and I want you to know this friendship is important to me. I don't think I'd have survived the last few, well, years without you."

"So, we're good?" Mike asked.

"Yeah, we're good, but know that my feelings aren't going to fade away easily, okay?" Mackenzie said. "You made it really seem like you liked me with the outfit matching, inviting me to dinner as the only two single people, and, well, all the support and what I thought was flirting…"

Mackenzie wiped a tear from her eye. Mike hugged her.

"I'm sorry. I never intended for any of that to give you the wrong signals. I thought I was being friendly. But know I'm not going anywhere."

The two stopped hugging and stood in silence for a minute before Mike left. Mackenzie waited for his car to leave the parking lot before running to her family's van to cry tears of relief that he finally told her how he felt.

Chapter Fifty

"So, he said no, he doesn't feel the same way, which means we're in the clear with Rachel now, right?" Serena asked Mackenzie that night as they did homework at the former's house.

"I feel like she would still be pissed," Mackenzie said. "I never told her I had feelings and made a huge love confession to him."

"True, but should you be worried?" Serena asked.

"This is Rachel, she'll get mad to find out that I confessed to him then went to a concert with him. She'll see it as a date."

"But it's not going to be a date. Just tell her it's platonic."

"I can tell her we're just friends and she'd trust that, but she already seems suspicious of me the last few weeks. It's like I'm already dating him minus the actual relationship, which she doesn't have. She'll be mad. I still have feelings for him too."

"But you can't help that," Serena said. "She knows you guys are just friends regardless. How do we even know she still has feelings for Mike? She hasn't talked to him in a while. I haven't noticed her rambling about him during choir lately."

"I don't want to get caught up in it," Mackenzie said as she stared at their AP Government practice test questions. "Is there any way you could ask her if she still has feelings for him?"

"Why?" Serena asked, confused.

"Because it will sound more legit since you guys aren't as close and you're trying to catch up or make up with her for whatever she's now mad at you about. Also, you're most likely to question everything she does."

"Okay, but I'm doing this for you," Serena said, staring at her textbook.

*** *** ***

Serena did not want to talk to Rachel. The two had just fought about AP class difficulty levels, how hard it is getting into schools, and what mattered on college applications. She was ready to cut her losses and move on to college. But she was asking Rachel about Mike for Mackenzie's sake, she reminded herself. This was for her friend who treated her like an equal. The next day before choir, Serena looked at Rachel and skipped her usual small talk as she took her seat.

"So, Rachel, where are you applying to college?" Serena said.

"Other than Cornell?" Rachel asked.

"Yeah."

"Well, I want to keep my options open, so I also applied to Loyola, Georgia Tech, Agnes Scott College, Carnegie Mellon, and Boston University."

"That's a lot of colleges," Serena said, wondering where she was going to go with this.

She couldn't have outright asked Rachel if she liked Mike, it would have tipped her off too easily.

"Well, my parents say the world is mine for the taking, so might as well try them all." Rachel smirked.

"Why those colleges specifically?" Serena asked nervously.

"Agnes Scott offers good scholarships and would be easy to transfer to Georgia Tech in the off chance I don't get in there. My family has some ties to Boston and BU is an excellent school. Carnegie Mellon is also a good school, and I can see myself living in Pittsburgh. And Loyola…" Rachel sighed. "Well, Mike is also applying to Loyola, so you know…"

"So, you still like him?" Serena interrupted.

"Yeah, why do you ask?"

"Well, I haven't seen you guys talk much lately, so I was just curious," Serena said quickly.

"Yeah, life, as you know, has been busy for us seniors," Rachel said. "But hopefully he'll be free for homecoming. I'll have to ask him to the dance."

"Yeah, you can do that!" Serena said, wanting to move on.

"What are your homecoming plans? There's no Luke Jackson to ask to dance with this year."

"I mean, Luke's fall break lines up with homecoming, but I figured I'd just go with you and Mackenzie and have fun, since it's a semiformal."

"Oh, so you're—" Rachel was cut off by the morning bell. Everyone got up for morning prayer, the Pledge of Allegiance, attendance, and uniform inspections.

Rachel was confused about what was suddenly happening. She hadn't spoken so openly to Serena in a while, and she wasn't mad at her anymore. She cooled off from their last argument. But Serena suddenly asked her about Mike, which she hadn't done in a long while. Also, Mackenzie was acting skittish around the school. She didn't feel jealous of Mackenzie, but the girl was acting weird that one day after the football game with Mike. Were they doing something behind her back? Like scheming to get Mike and Mackenzie together? But that didn't make sense, especially adding to the fact that asking a friend about colleges isn't suspicious. But still, something weird was going on and Rachel was feeling jealousy bubble up in her.

It's probably nothing, she told herself. But thinking about it made her more upset. Mackenzie naturally was able to spend more time with Mike. Rachel just wouldn't be able to get as close. She then remembered that the duo was going to a concert this weekend as well. Mackenzie said to not worry because Mike sees her as a friend. But did Rachel trust Mackenzie?

Chapter Fifty-One

"Ready?" Mike asked as Mackenzie buckled her seatbelt in Shirleen that Saturday.

"Is Kevin Scarpino hot?" she asked him.

"I don't know, is he?" Mike replied.

"Mike, we discussed this. I sent you links to his stuff; you were supposed to stream."

"I did." He swiped at his phone, and Scarpino's "Twisted Memories" started playing as they took off.

"You jerk." Mackenzie punched his arm.

"Watch it. I'm driving," Mike said.

"Sorry."

"No, I'm kidding." He slugged her back before merging into a lane.

The hour trip to the concert venue flew by for the two as Mackenzie tried her best not to belt out Scarpino's music before the concert. Mike hummed along.

Both were feeling a lot better after talking out their feelings a few days ago. Mackenzie was sad he didn't reciprocate them, but she was getting better each day. She told herself she was never going to get over him, but maybe that was fine as long as they were able to talk. She could lose her crush eventually, but not her friend.

As they pulled into the venue parking lot, Mackenzie surprised him with VIP passes she won in a random drawing, and they got to go backstage to meet Scarpino before the concert. Mike and Mackenzie were both impressed with the budding artist. He had a clean dressing room with scented candles, and his clothes were neat. He spoke softly to save his voice for the show.

"She's doing that to save hers too," Mike whispered. That made the artist laugh.

"So, you guys are big fans then?"

"She's listened to you nonstop since the summer," Mike answered. "She'll casually drop your lyrics into a conversation or in our class essays."

"Not true!" Mackenzie squeaked while blushing.

"That's awesome!" Scarpino said. "What's your guy's names?"

"I'm Mackenzie," she said, feeling her face go red. "This is my friend, Mike."

"Well, thanks again for coming to the show," he started. "Want to take pictures?"

Mackenzie almost dropped her phone at his suggestion, but they were able to recover it and do shots of them arm in arm and then silly faces. After taking posed photos with him, Mackenzie was already on a concert high.

"Well, that was nice," Mike said as they took their seats. "Do you think he found us creepy?"

"Probably just you." Mackenzie smiled.

"Hey, I'm not the one who barely spoke to him."

"I'm saving my voice, you jerk!"

"Think of me as your wingman," Mike said. "I was just helping you. Maybe he'll ask for your number after the show."

Mackenzie laughed.

"I doubt that... Wait, do you really think he would?"

Soon after, the concert started. Mackenzie, like all the rest of the girls there, screamed for Kevin Scarpino, took photos and videos of his songs, and swayed to the music. She was happy she could get Mike to at least dance to the last song, "If You Won't", with her.

"Okay that was awesome," Mike said as they left for his car. "Who knew brand new artists could be fun?"

Mackenzie laughed and shook her head. As they drove away, Mike was quiet for five minutes in thought.

"What's up?" Mackenzie asked him.

"Hey, I need you to know, and I hope this doesn't bring down your mood, but I'm taking someone with me to homecoming next week."

Mackenzie paused.

"Ok." She nodded.

"I met her at the river cleanup last spring. I asked her to the dance a few days before you ran to my house. I really hope this doesn't make things more awkward between us. If it helps, I think she goes to school with your friend Michelle."

Mackenzie was riding the concert high too much to let this news break her. Kevin Scarpino is once in a lifetime. But Mike's words would probably hurt when she's calmed down.

"I mean, is anything going to be more awkward than me running to your house at night?" Mackenzie said.

"Fair enough." Mike shrugged. "I didn't just ruin your night, did I?"

"No," Mackenzie said as she played more Kevin Scarpino on her phone.

After they got home, Mackenzie uploaded her photos and videos onto her social media. Her smile couldn't leave her face. She went with Mike to see a sweet performer who blew the roof off the house. She uploaded five pics of her and Mike with Kevin doing silly faces; Kevin was humble enough to take photos with them and complied with their face and pose requests.

✶ ✶ ✶

Rachel was home from the opera that night when she went on social media and saw all the photos and videos Mackenzie posted. At first, she liked them. Then she saw how much fun it looked like Mackenzie and Mike had. She had fun at the opera, but she saw the joy in Mike and Mackenzie's (and possibly Kevin Scarpino's) eyes. She was jealous. She admitted to herself that even as she attempted to live her best life, others were also killing it. Mike and Mackenzie were also super close in that photo. They couldn't be in love. But also, what if they were?

"Looks like fun!" she commented on one of Mackenzie's photos. Twenty minutes later, Mackenzie liked the comment.

Rachel decided to text her.

Rachel: How was the concert with Mike?

Mackenzie: We had a lot of fun 😊

Rachel: Was the drive long?

Mackenzie: Not when you're singing indie rock by a beautiful soul-voiced man

Rachel rolled her eyes. At least Kevin Scarpino wasn't in high school with them.

Rachel: Did Mike like him?

Mackenzie: He did surprisingly 😊

Rachel: Did you guys do anything after the concert?

Mackenzie: He just drove me home, but since we got to the venue early, we got fast food

Not romantic food at least.

Rachel: Did he pay?

She sent that without thinking.

"Why?" Mackenzie heard herself say out loud.

Mackenzie held her phone carefully while in bed. She was confused for a minute before seeing through the jealousy. She immediately went on the defensive.

"No," she immediately replied which was a lie.

Mike knew Mackenzie was low on funds and bought her dinner.

Mackenzie: But we talked for a while on the way home about homecoming. I guess he really wants to dance with someone he knows well

That was true, but Mackenzie had a strong feeling Mike wasn't talking about either of them.

Rachel: Who?

Mackenzie: Some girl. He didn't tell me.

Mackenzie then hid her phone in her desk drawer to avoid Rachel's investigations for the night. She wasn't going to let Rachel's investigations ruin her night. Not after she met her low-rung celebrity crush.

Rachel, on the other hand, was annoyed. She didn't get anything from the conversation other than Mike and Mackenzie went Dutch on their date. She also realized Mackenzie was not going to help her with that last text. When did Mackenzie get so evasive? Also, who was this girl none of them knew? Something was up, and Rachel just wanted to get to homecoming next week to get to the bottom of everything.

Chapter Fifty-Two

Rachel saw homecoming as her final shot with Mike. It was do or die time in her mind. Rachel's heart was pounding at the thought of asking Mike out, but she knew it'd be a waste to worry and then not shoot her shot. Rachel poked Mike a little too hard on the shoulder after AP Calc that Monday.

"Sorry," Rachel said as she picked up her books. "I was going to ask are you taking anyone to homecoming?"

"Actually, I am." Mike smiled.

"Oh okay," Rachel said.

Well, she thought, *at least he isn't dating Mackenzie.*

"Wait, who are you taking?" Rachel said, shocked.

"She doesn't go here. She's a friend from community service projects. We've cleaned up the river together."

"Okay well, I look forward to meeting her on Saturday."

For the rest of the day, Rachel couldn't stop thinking about Mike's date for Saturday. Who was this girl? Since when did Mike talk to people outside his circle? Also, how could she be well suited for Mike if she didn't know what was going on in his life? Well, they regularly communicated and she heard some of his tales about life outside of St. Joseph's. Rachel was so convinced she and Mike were right together it was terrifying to think she was wrong. All of her time in high school would have been wasted. After school, she walked up to Mackenzie and told her about Mike's date.

"Yeah, it's weird," Mackenzie said.

"What are we going to do?" Rachel asked.

"Um, invite them to hang out with us at the dance," Mackenzie suggested.

As unenthused as she was about Mike liking another girl she wouldn't let on her own feelings.

"Yeah, I guess so. What if his date is so much better than me?" Rachel asked.

"She's not. You're pretty awesome in your own right," Mackenzie said while resisting the urge to roll her eyes.

Mackenzie packed her backpack and hurried. She still liked Mike, and it was hard to know he liked someone else while her delusional friend thought she was the only one who was going through heartbreak.

"Well, I'll see you later." Mackenzie rushed out.

✷ ✷ ✷

That Saturday, Mackenzie arrived at homecoming twenty minutes late to find Rachel, Serena, and Michelle, who Serena took as her guest, dancing to pop music.

"HEY!" they all hugged her above the loud music.

Everything seemed to go right, although Mackenzie noticed some death glares from a few classmates and Ron. She hadn't thought about him in a while and was surprised he was there considering he threw five interceptions and got sacked twice, leading to a blowout loss the night before.

After a few minutes, the girls heard Mike shouting.

"HI EVERYONE, THIS IS DOLLY SPRAGGINS."

Mackenzie and Rachel turned around to meet Mike and his date. Dolly was five-two and had already kicked off her heels. With her green satin dress reflecting in the strobe light and light blond hair styled in a bob, everyone was suddenly envious of her beauty. Mike complimented her outfit with a matching green tie and a nice black suit.

"Hi." Dolly waved.

"WHAT?" Rachel and Mackenzie yelled.

"HI," Dolly yelled back.

"SO HOW DID YOU GUYS MEET?" Serena asked.

"WE WERE CLEANING THE RIVER AND STARTED TALKING—" Dolly was cut off by a slow song starting.

Dolly and Mike broke off to start dancing. Michelle and Serena were approached by some senior soccer players. Rachel and Mackenzie stood off to the side of the gym as they watched the couples dance. Both were envious as Mike put his hands low on Dolly's waist. She was small, which added to the awkwardness of Mike's height, but the couple didn't seem to notice. They watched them talk and at some point, Mike laughed loudly. After the song was over, everyone regrouped.

"THAT WAS FUN," Michelle said first.

"YEAH, ESPECIALLY STANDING IN THE CORNER," Rachel said sharply.

"ARE YOU OKAY?" Serena shouted.

"I'M FINE."

Rachel walked off as the rest of the group continued to dance. Rachel went to cool off in the bathroom. *Don't be jealous, don't be jealous, don't be jealous,* she kept telling herself as she walked back and forth across the stalls. She was still angry when she went to the snack table and had some punch. *Why is it after three years he can't take a hint?* Rachel thought. She wound herself back up again.

After another half hour of deliberating, she went back to the dance floor where a cheesy slow song was playing. Her jaw dropped as she saw Mike now slow dance with Mackenzie. Rachel felt her anger come back. She masked it with a smile and walked up to Dolly who was watching.

"WHAT ARE YOU DOING? ISN'T HE YOUR DATE?" Rachel yelled.

"YEAH, BUT THEY'RE GOOD FRIENDS SO I FIGURED WHY NOT," Dolly said. "MIKE TALKS ABOUT THEIR FRIENDSHIP A LOT, AND I NOTICED SHE DIDN'T HAVE A PARTNER AT THE LAST SONG."

Rachel was officially over this dance. She kindly said it was nice to meet Dolly and then left the dance floor again. Her friends eventually noticed she was missing, but Mackenzie and Serena knew talking to her would make things worse. They decided to wait until after the dance and after Mike and Dolly left to invite her to a sleepover.

***

At Serena's house, they listened to an hour-long rant about Dolly. Everything Rachel said about Mike being a flake and suddenly liking someone out of the blue was completely random and disappointing, which Mackenzie agreed with but kept her mouth shut.

"Who does that to someone? Who acts so friendly and then so oblivious? And then Dolly has him dance with you but not me? What is up with that?" Rachel complained to Mackenzie.

"They couldn't find you for the next slow song," Michelle said quietly.

She didn't know much about the dating drama since their junior year of high school and didn't care since her school had its own drama. However, what she said was true, Mike was looking for Rachel when she was in the bathroom cooling down for a second time.

Rachel was mad but couldn't go ballistic on Michelle. She realized how ridiculous it was and stopped talking for half an hour while the rest of the girls discussed the dance, the lousy football team this year, and Michelle's public school.

"So, do they really not allow flannel at public school?" Serena asked Michelle.

"They think flannel is another form of pajamas, so no," Michelle responded.

"That's ridiculous."

"Tell me about it."

Rachel took some deep breaths in and out. It was pointless to get mad here considering none of them did anything with Mike. Mackenzie wasn't his date, but she was annoyed at the thought of them dancing. Probably because they were close and seemed to be having fun. She just wanted that with him. As she lay on an air mattress, she closed her eyes. *It's okay if you are jealous, don't lash out,* she kept internally telling herself as she slowed her breathing.

Chapter Fifty-Three

The more Rachel thought about her feelings, the more she became annoyed with the world around her. She decided to keep away from her friends to feel better. While everyone was getting ready for the senior night game, Mike was starting to text her more often asking if she was going to attend. That made her feel better, but she didn't want to see him with Dolly or Mackenzie. She was a little mad at him for ignoring her until this week. It wasn't until Thursday she finally relented to go to the game due to Mike's bribery.

Rachel: Please help me with problem 7 for AP Calculus.

Mike: Sure, but there's one condition

Rachel: Okay, what?

Mike: Go to the pregame ceremony for the senior game

Rachel: Okay.

Mike: Well, that was easy

Rachel smiled at his text; he got her good. Thankfully, he helped her with the problem, which when she checked afterward, was correct. Rachel found herself in the football stands with Serena that Friday night before the last game.

"I can't believe it's senior night," Rachel said. "We've almost made it."

"Yeah, I'm just happy we've gotten to tonight," Serena said. "The last few weeks have been tough."

That Friday pre-game ceremony started with the recognition of the senior football players, cheerleaders, majorettes, and band members. The senior band members led the national anthem and school song. Mike and Mackenzie stood next to each other for the performances, and Rachel noticed Mike whisper something into her ear as the John Paul Eagle's lineup was announced. Mackenzie broke out in a smile. It was just friendliness, Rachel reminded herself.

After the band cleared the field, the game started. The Lancers were bad this year, and everyone attending the game was only there to support the seniors. Surprisingly, what started as an 0-16 beating in the first half turned into a last-minute victory for St. Joseph's. The Lancers caught a pick in the third quarter that propelled them into a tie in the last five minutes of the game. After rushing to the 20-yard line at the end of the game, the Lancers were on fourth down and looked to set up a field goal. Instead of following through, the team broke out and threw a touchdown, winning 22-16. Everyone in the crowd went nuts. The football team poured their ice water on Coach Dobbs, the cheerleaders jumped up and down, and the band played rapidly.

After the game was over, the girls caught up with their friends in the band room. Rachel was happy until she saw Mike and Mackenzie give each other a tight hug.

"Hey, how's it going?" she interrupted.

"We won!" Mackenzie and Mike jumped up and down. They all high fived.

"It's like I said earlier before the game, act stupid enough and the football team will win," Mike said to Mackenzie.

"No, you said if we won, you would shave your head." Mackenzie laughed.

"That's bad. I would miss your hair," Rachel said.

Mike ignored her.

"No, I said your head." He joked as he grabbed Mackenzie's ponytail. "Say goodbye to these pretty locks."

"Eh, it's just hair." Mackenzie shrugged.

"It's long and shiny."

Rachel left the band room, annoyed.

***

As she laid in bed, she kept thinking about Mike and Mackenzie being so close at the game. It bothered her that he was flirting with her after the game. But then again, it seemed like this wasn't the first time she saw them flirt. It seemed like something was up with them since junior year. Mike took Mackenzie to weekly dinners with two priesthood discerning high school boys. That was odd. Then, as Serena mentioned months ago, he just happened to match her at the prom, which he did with Dolly. Dolly was also cool enough to let Mackenzie dance with him, which was weird since she was his date. As weird as that was, Rachel ignored Dolly since it didn't fit in with her current train of thought.

A few weeks before the dance, Serena randomly asked her if she still liked Mike. She and Serena weren't that close this year, but suddenly asking her about her feelings was out of the blue. Serena also was supposed to be studying with Mackenzie when her phone happened to still be at home. What if the three of them were hanging out or she stayed at Mackenzie's house while she snuck out to see him. Also, Mike seemed to have gotten more protective of Mackenzie after she broke up with Ron.

Okay, something is wrong, Rachel thought. *My best friend and crush are suspiciously close, they danced together at homecoming, and he literally flirted with her right in front of me. They like each other and are probably secretly dating. They're doing this as a secret because she knows I get jealous and didn't want me to blow up. But if she didn't want me to, then she shouldn't have gone behind my back! This friendship is as messed up as the day she asked him out and told him to keep it secret.*

Rachel opened her eyes and texted Mackenzie.

Rachel: Hey.

She waited half an hour for a response but didn't get anything. After waking up the next day, she checked her phone. Still nothing.

Rachel: We need to talk.

Mackenzie didn't text back at all. She wasn't stupid. She knew Rachel was mad about Friday night, and she had a feeling she would get an earful if she messaged back. So, she didn't respond, which only enraged Rachel more. Before she got another text, Mackenzie turned off her phone for the weekend.

If Mondays were not already hard enough, this one was going to be terrible. Mackenzie couldn't sleep Sunday night, knowing what was coming the next day. Rachel was home telling herself not to be jealous but knew she was going to bring this all up the next day. She knew she wouldn't be able to contain it all when she saw Mackenzie, so she prayed she could be nice about it.

Chapter Fifty-Four

Mackenzie was unpacking at her locker quickly in an attempt to avoid Rachel's interactions that morning. She was two steps past her locker when Rachel jumped in front of her.

"Hey," Rachel said eagerly.

Mackenzie tried to move sideways, but Rachel seemed to be blocking her path with the flow of student traffic.

"Hey, Rachel, what's up?"

"Why didn't you respond to my texts this weekend?" Rachel cut off the small talk.

"My phone died, and I couldn't find the charger," Mackenzie lied.

"Don't you have a lot of chargers since you have a big family?"

"You'd be surprised."

"Well, I'm not surprised that you're avoiding me. I know what you're hiding."

Mackenzie stared at Rachel as her heart dropped a few stories.

"I know about you and Mike," she said softly.

"What?"

"I know you guys are dating," she said louder.

"Mike and I are not dating," Mackenzie said truthfully.

"Stop lying!" Rachel yelled. "You know I hate lying. You have been seeing him behind my back this year, you slut!"

Rachel was furious.

"You know I like him and you still went behind my back. Who the hell do you think you are!" Rachel continued.

Mackenzie was leaning back from how forceful Rachel was shouting. A few students around them stopped and stared. Teachers were starting to notice the hallway's unusually raucous volume.

"And what the hell was with you doing it with that fake, two-faced Serena!" Rachel shouted. "You turned her against me! You ruined two friendships with your backstabbing ways! I trusted you! I had faith in our friendship, but I guess that's what happens when you make friends with backstabbing sluts."

"I didn't do anything to Serena!" Mackenzie found herself yelling back. "She made her own decisions. How many times do I have to tell you I'm not dating Mike? If you were a good friend, shouldn't you have trusted us anyways?!"

Mackenzie was surprised she found herself arguing back with Rachel.

"We made a pact!"

"It was a stupid pact we made two years ago while on stupid o'clock because you're insecure and jealous about everything!" Mackenzie yelled back. "If you didn't want to get so upset, maybe you should have asked him out instead of asking us to help you. Have you ever thought that maybe your attempts to get with him weren't working BECAUSE HE DIDN'T LIKE YOU?"

"He didn't like me because YOU STOLE HIM!"

"No, he didn't like you because YOU'RE NOT APPEALING!"

Rachel lunged at Mackenzie, taking her down with her books. After struggling for a moment, Mackenzie found herself pulled away by some wrestling team members. Math teachers Mr. Bill O'Connor and Dr. George Trey held Rachel back while she kept swiping.

"DON'T THINK OUR FRIENDSHIP STILL EXISTS!" Rachel yelled as she was pulled to the front office.

Mackenzie was pulled into Miss Smith's empty classroom to cool off. She had a planning period and closed the door.

"Are you okay? What happened, Mackenzie?"

"I don't know. She got mad and lunged at me." Mackenzie started sobbing, feeling for cuts on her face.

"Why was she mad at you?" Ms. Lawson said as she prepared a washcloth.

"Well, it's kind of a long story that started sophomore year," Mackenzie felt tears well in her eyes. "We made this pact about dating guys and …"

✼ ✼ ✼

Rachel was fuming in Principal Sister Mary Jo's office as she called her parents to come over.

"I didn't do anything wrong. She betrayed me," Rachel said as she sobbed. "She took him from me!"

Her parents argued her case that Rachel was a good student, had good grades, and was involved in activities, so she shouldn't be punished, or else it may affect her college applications. If anything, Rachel had been working on her jealousy issues and was channeling it into her music lessons. Sister Mary Jo understood but also knew the school policy. Rachel was handed three days of out of school suspension for her actions.

After she and her parents left the school, Mackenzie was called to the principal's office to talk about what happened. Visibly upset, Mackenzie felt herself shaking as she talked to Sister Mary Jo.

"We had made this pact that if a guy came between us and was better for one friend than the other than we would stop being friends. I didn't mean to upset her, and I didn't steal Mike if that's what she told you."

"We believe you, Miss Bishop." Sister Mary Jo sighed.

Mackenzie's parents let her leave school for the day. While at home, Mackenzie just sat there, not sure what to do. She turned on her phone to see over twenty texts from Rachel from the weekend, each one angrier than the last. Mackenzie was glad none were from today, but when she was on social media, she noticed Rachel unfollowed and unfriended her on all mediums.

Every student who was upstairs when the commotion broke out didn't know what happened until lunch. Serena and Mike figured Mackenzie was sick in AP Government that morning. In the cafeteria, Serena looked around for Mackenzie but couldn't find her friend. Mike called her over to his table with fellow trombone players.

"Hey, have you seen Mackenzie?" she asked as she put her tray down on the table.

"She left early. Apparently, she and Rachel got into a fight," Mike said calmly.

"Oh no," Serena groaned, realizing Rachel knew about Mackenzie's feelings.

"Do you know what it was about?" Mike asked.

"Did Rachel swing first?" Dave asked.

"It's… complicated," Serena said. "Just be nice to them both, okay?"

"Why wouldn't I?" Mike asked, confused.

Serena didn't want to spread more gossip through the school, so she dug through her lunch and let Dave and Kevin talk about their classes and what they heard about the fight.

***

Mackenzie showed up to school the next day, wanting to turn invisible. Serena texted her the night before that people were spreading rumors about the fight, one saying she had further brain damage in addition to her concussion and was sent to an institution. As she opened her locker, she saw the photo from freshman year of her, Rachel and Serena. She took it off of the magnets holding it and stared at it for a minute. Mackenzie then tore it into two pieces and threw it in the nearest trash can. Rachel said their friendship was over, so it didn't matter.

Mackenzie walked to class, wanting to hide at the art table as Mike sat across from her.

"Hey, Mackenzie," he began.

"Hey," she murmured.

"I don't know what happened yesterday, but are you feeling better?"

"Yeah, I'll be all right."

No one else sat at the table with them. Mike and Serena made sure to sit with her at lunch to make her feel better. Then Mike approached her at her car after school.

"Are you sure you're okay?" he asked.

"I'm almost feeling better," Mackenzie said.

"Why's that?" Mike asked.

"It's kind of complicated."

"Like what?"

"You really want to know?"

"Yeah, why not?"

"It kind of involves you."

"Well, now I want to know. Tell me!"

"Okay, but this may take a while," Mackenzie said. "Can we get in my car for more privacy?"

Mike was already pulling at the passenger door. Once inside, he put on his seat belt.

"Okay, I'm buckled up for this wild ride," he joked.

"I'm glad." Mackenzie smiled. "So, the story starts summer before sophomore year."

Chapter Fifty-Five

Rachel returned to St. Joseph's the next week after taking another two days off from school after her suspension was up. She refused to talk to Mackenzie after having to formally apologize to her in person and in a letter as demanded by the administration. Mackenzie wouldn't make eye contact with her in Sister Mary Jo's office and seemed to mumble "thanks" before taking the letter from Rachel's hands.

Rachel didn't want to try with Serena. She didn't need to apologize to her but knew Serena wouldn't want to talk to her. She blocked her on all forms of social media anyway.

Rachel didn't want to sit near Mike in class that week either. Someone probably told him she liked him and that she went psycho on one of his closest friends. Rachel decided the best route to deal with everyone was to ignore the problem and cut her losses from everyone. She walked to class with her head high and asked Mrs. Krammer if she could switch seats in AP Calculus, which was granted.

As Rachel took her seats for her classes the next few days, she noticed no one would sit next to her unless a teacher complained about the awkward seating arrangement. After a week of self-isolation, Rachel attempted to sit next to Serena in choir.

"How has choir been?" Rachel asked.

"Good, nothing new," Serena said.

"Have the altos finally learned their part?"

Serena nodded. Mrs. King cut Rachel off and started class. Nothing was hard for Rachel to catch up with schoolwork-wise. But it seemed like everyone who personally knew Rachel left her alone. Even the sopranos seemed to give Rachel the cold shoulder. Everyone in Christian Vocations would bring up jealousy and obedience as if on purpose when talking about religious lifestyles they were learning about. No one would partner with her in her AP Physics lab. Rachel started eating alone at lunch. It seemed like Father Jack's homilies were starting to be about students getting along and treating each other with respect.

Rachel was ready to quit. It was her senior year, the supposed peak of high school, but no one would approach her. She just wanted to fast forward through the year so she could graduate and move on. The only people who seemed to be nice to her were the freshmen in her elective classes, but she wasn't sure if that was out of duty or them being genuine.

It was around Thanksgiving as she was packing up after AP Calc when Mike finally approached her.

"Hey, Rachel," he began.

Rachel was surprised to see him talk to her.

"Hey!" She smiled, a little too eager to have someone seek her out.

"Are you free after school today?"

"Yeah, what's up?"

"Just want to talk for a few minutes," he said.

"I can do that."

There was a bright spot in Rachel's day. He would at least tell her he still accepted her. Maybe even tell her she's a good person or he would still be her friend. She knew it was too much to daydream that Mike would ask her out later, but she wanted it to be a possibility.

After class, she met him at the benches in front of the school. Mike approached Rachel slowly.

"Are you okay?" she asked him, anxious for the conversation to begin.

"Yeah, it's just hard for me to be serious," he said as he sat down next to her.

"So, what do you want to talk about?"

"I know you like me, Rachel," Mike said.

Rachel froze.

"Mackenzie told me everything after that fight you had with her. Listen, I'm sorry, but I don't feel the same way. I should have known you liked me since sophomore year, but I was too oblivious. I only saw you as a friend then and still do. I heard you get jealous easily, but you need to know I don't like Mackenzie romantically either. She's like a sister to me with how close we are. We are good friends; I never meant for it to look like we were dating. I think she misunderstood all of my actions too. The girls at this school are nice, but I've never wanted to date anyone here.

"I met Dolly last year when getting service hours for graduation, and she's such a sweet person, I feel lucky to know her. She was not a plant to make anyone jealous. I was surprised when she told me to dance with you guys, but I thought it was sweet. She's a great girl, but ironically, I don't think she likes me back.

"None of this was meant to hurt you, and I'm sorry if I lead you on. That was never my intention. I didn't realize your crush until it was too late, and now it's kind of ruined everything. I feel—"

Rachel cut him off as she stared at the ground. "You didn't ruin anything. It's not your fault."

"Maybe," Mike continued. "But you don't need to punish yourself or stop being friends with me. I kind of want to move on and have fun for the rest of the year."

"Yeah?" Rachel raised her head.

"And also, not feel pressured to text you AP Calc questions."

Rachel started tearing up.

"I'm sorry. I feel so foolish about everything that's happened. I should have stopped lying to myself during junior year about you liking me. It was so obvious you didn't and I took it out on others. I'm sorry you had to watch me act at my lowest form of decency. But everything I did was for you, and I was so confused, from driving with you after pit rehearsal, to joining a community band and always asking about your weekend plans. All of my school dance schemes seemed to fall apart by illnesses or family emergencies. It was all for nothing."

Rachel's tears were going down her cheeks now.

"And the hardest part was I really struggle with my jealousy, and I kept telling myself to control it and to hold it in. I tried meditating and learning techniques to stay calm, but no matter what, I'll now be known as the girl who went psycho on her former best friend in the hallways. No one wants to associate with me anymore. I should have known I couldn't keep it bottled up forever. This is what I get, no one and nothing!"

Rachel continued loudly sobbing for a few minutes. Mike patted the back of her shoulder after a while.

"Hey, it sucks, but I'm here as a friend," Mike said. "What you did was stupid, but we all deserve second chances."

"Thanks," Rachel choked. "Why are you being so nice to me?"

"Well, you can't be a loner," Mike explained. "That's not nice. No one should be ashamed forever. Look at me, I was a partier who got in trouble, then a loner who found out having no friends at all was worse. Also, again, I still need help with math homework, and you get back to me pretty quickly when I text you questions."

"Thanks for understanding." Rachel stopped crying. Rachel and Mike awkwardly hugged each other.

Chapter Fifty-Six

Rachel was surprised her wish for the school year to fly came true. Time seemed to speed up after Thanksgiving. Winter midterms were approaching, and everyone was stressed as usual. Slowly, more and more people started talking to her again before Christmas. After the school's winter music concert, every soprano one was thankful for her helping keep a D above the staff for six measures.

"Good job." Mary Kate Love made the effort to compliment her.

Rachel took the small compliment to heart.

Her AP Calc classmates were suddenly asking for her to organize a study group again. Mike helped her reserve tables at the library for the group. Rachel was astounded by how many classmates showed up and turned to her for answers.

"According to my parents, if I don't get a ninety five or above on this exam, I can't go to prom," Mike explained. "I raised the bar too much last year."

"Yeah, I have a feeling you won't be going," Rachel replied.

The winter midterms melted into Christmas and Rachel went skiing with her parents in Vail again. She was happy to just have a text from Mike wishing her a Merry Christmas.

After the return from break, more classmates were open to talking to her again. She found lunch tables with classmates and felt like she could finally breathe. Rachel was relieved to be accepted again.

The next semester, she didn't have lunch with any of her original friends but sat with some nice underclassmen who seemed to forget or not know the hallway debacle she had months earlier with Mackenzie.

January became February and everyone was spending money on carnation sales again. She sent one to Mike for his generosity and got one back from him. Before everyone at the school knew it, the month skipped to March and every senior was freaking out about college acceptance and rejection letters. Rachel was nervous since she had the school suspension on her record but was hopeful she could still get into most of her schools.

Mackenzie and Mike both got rejected by Harvard, which surprised neither of them. They ended up signing each other's letters and hanging them in their lockers. Mike was accepted to Loyola and was happy his family said they could afford it. Mackenzie was rejected by the University of Chicago but got into her other schools, Georgia Southern and Agnes Scott. She was upset about Georgia Southern's financial package not offering much unless she wanted to drown in loans, but knew she was going to end up at Agnes Scott which she was happy with since she got an almost full ride there.

Mackenzie was happy with her decision until she heard Rachel was offered a full ride there. Rachel wasn't happy about it either since Cornell, Boston University, Georgia Tech, and Carnegie Mellon rejected her. Loyola waitlisted her as she watched other classmates celebrate getting in. So, Agnes Scott it was for her if she wanted to transfer to Georgia Tech.

One day in April, she ran into Mackenzie in the bathroom during a school retreat. Neither spoke for a minute.

"So, I heard you got into Agnes Scott," Rachel started.

Mackenzie didn't respond as she washed her hands.

"I'm going there too because of the scholarship. Wouldn't it be funny if we got paired as roommates or something?"

Mackenzie dried her hands and left the bathroom. As she left, Serena entered the bathroom to rinse out a contact lens.

"Hey, Serena, congrats on getting into William and Mary."

"Thanks," she said curtly as she pulled her contact out of her left eye.

"Why are you guys being like this?"

"Like what?"

Serena carefully washed her contact under a light stream of water.

"Why are you and Mackenzie being such jerks and blowing me off! I'm trying to talk to you."

"Seriously, Rachel?" Serena reinserted the contact in her eye. "You're not a nice person. You never apologized to me about calling me a slut in the hall. You haven't even tried sincerely making up to Mackenzie considering you jumped on her and yelled at her. You only apologized to her because the administration made you. We're not the jerks here."

Serena stared at her eye in the mirror before walking out of the bathroom. Rachel was stunned for the rest of the day. She knew she was abrasive, but she didn't think she had to apologize again. She was over her angry feelings and figured everyone else moved on. As she sat at adoration that day, she started feeling sorry for herself. She didn't mean to cause so much pain, and she felt bad for being the villain this time. This drama started because she caused it. She dared to ignore it and only feel sorry for Mike after it all happened. She never considered Serena was also affected by her actions. She figured the forced apology to Mackenzie closed that door. She knew her jealousy hurt herself but didn't think about how it hurt everyone around her.

Rachel hated apologizing. Her parents always told her she was right and to stand her ground in any conflict. Her family was never one to argue often or get into conflicts, so she never saw her parents do much of it. After the retreat that day, she was scared of trying to apologize. She decided to start small and text Mackenzie and Serena in their old group chat.

Rachel: Hey guys, I'm sorry about the last few months. I've been so rude. I never knew my actions were affecting others hard, and I don't want to end our senior year on a sour note.

Serena read the message, but no notifications showed Mackenzie saw it. That was because Mackenzie was done with Rachel's crap and blocked her on all communication platforms. Knowing she was going to have to suck it up and say it in person, Rachel texted Mike for advice.

Rachel: Should I apologize to them face to face?
Mike: Yes
Rachel: You don't know who I'm texting about.
Mike: Yeah, I do. Mack and Serena.
Rachel: Why didn't you tell me I should have done this earlier?
Mike: That's your responsibility to know, not mine :/

Rachel sighed. He was right, but she still didn't want to do it.

✱✱✱

The next Monday, she tried to avoid getting to school on time so she wouldn't have to apologize so soon. But her car didn't face any red lights in the city. She was there twenty minutes before the first-class bell rang. Her feet couldn't stop moving until she was right in front of Serena and Mackenzie's lockers.

"Hey," she said quietly while the two were taking books out. They didn't hear her.

"Uh hey, Mackenzie, Serena," Rachel started again.

They turned around.

"Listen, I'm sorry about all I've done. I'm sorry about yelling and calling you names. Mackenzie, I'm sorry I attacked you and that I let my jealousy take advantage of me. Serena, I'm sorry I called you a slut and taking my anger out on you. You both don't deserve it. I was just projecting my crazy insecure thoughts on both of you. Could you please forgive me?"

"Fine," Serena said as she walked off.

Mackenzie stared at Rachel for a few seconds.

"I can forgive you, but that doesn't mean I want to be your friend again."

"Why not?" Rachel asked desperately. "We can rebuild our friendship and be better friends. I'm going to counseling now."

"You attacked me and got insane at me for nothing. I can forgive you, but I don't want to be buddy-buddy with you here or at Agnes Scott. I'll admit I was kinda wrong. I was lying by keeping my feelings to myself, but you're the one who actively tried to hurt me. There's no going forward as friends from that. You have to realize that."

Mackenzie closed her locker and walked to class. *At least I'm forgiven,* Rachel thought. At choir, Serena was now keeping her distance but not completely blocking her out. Rachel would accept that for now. Mackenzie was going to be harder to make up with.

***

After the Easter break, all the seniors were thrown into a head rush. AP exams were taken, and everyone got ready for prom. Mike took Dolly to the dance again, which Mackenzie and Rachel accepted. Mackenzie took Dave again, and Serena, to Mike's suprise and delight, took Kevin Fisher as her date. Rachel decided to not go to the dance. She didn't want to see Dolly there and feel jealous all over again. She accepted that while she liked Mike, it was going to be hard to get over him and didn't want her feelings to take over again.

With that, the days skipped to graduation. Valedictorian Katie Sims and salutatorian Brian Jenkins gave speeches on their time at St.

Joseph's. All the seniors walked across the stage to their families clapping, and caps were thrown at the end. Mike went around taking graduation selfies with everyone and reminded them about his party the next day.

When Rachel arrived at Mike's open house, it was already crowded with family she never met and classmates. She said hi to Mike and talked to him for ten minutes before he got pulled away by a great uncle. Rachel sighed and found herself at the snack table, getting guacamole and chips while Mackenzie was getting salsa.

"Hey," Rachel said.

"Hi." Mackenzie avoided eye contact.

"So, we did it."

"Yeah, it's pretty crazy we got here."

"We finally got to the end and now everyone is going their own ways."

"Well, not all of us," Mackenzie said. "We'll probably run into each other at Agnes Scott."

"Yeah? Do you think we'll have classes together?"

"Probably just intro stuff. I got accepted to the music program."

"Yeah, and I'll probably transfer to Georgia Tech after two years for their advanced STEM program."

"Really?"

"Yeah," Rachel affirmed. "You are friendly today. What changed?"

"You know, we're done with high school. We graduated and are starting our new lives. I don't need to worry about upsetting anyone anymore, and you apologized for attacking me, so it's time to move on."

"I'm glad." Rachel smiled. "I'm also sorry again for all of it. It was pretty stupid we made a pact that our friendship would be ruined if a guy was better for one person than another and he dates the second friend."

"I know! We ignored the hypothetical guy's feelings in all of it," Mackenzie agreed.

"We ignored Mike's feelings," they both said as they watched him talk to Dolly at the party.

"The pact was stupid," Mackenzie said. "Why would we be good friends if we said something could ruin our friendship? That's, like, setting up that it could get unhealthy."

"I should have realized it when I said it," Rachel said. "I'm sorry about all this."

"Don't worry about it. I was complicit," Mackenzie said.

"So, what now?" Rachel asked. "Are we friends again?"

"Maybe. But no more pacts."

Rachel laughed and agreed. The girls returned to a group forming with Mike, Serena, Dave, Kevin, and Dolly.

Repairing a burnt bridge takes a lot of work and whether these two were going to restore their friendship was up to how committed they felt. How Rachel used her fresh start and how she handled her jealousy were up to her at Agnes Scott. Mackenzie's assertiveness and confrontation skills were in her hands moving forward. But these things were far from their minds as Mackenzie and Rachel joked with their friends and ate their snacks.

The End.

Acknowledgements

I want to thank, first and foremost, you, the reader, for making it back here to the acknowledgments! Thank you for spending your time reading my debut novel by choice. *Mike in the Middle* has been a project in the making since 2019.

Thinking of 2019, I want to thank my now husband, Justin, for his steadfast support since we were dating for a month and a half while I started this book for NaNoWriMo. All of your wonderful encouragement while I wrote (and rewrote and rewrote) and sent to multiple publishers to starting up self-publishing is not lost on me. Every word in this book is for you.

So is every word also for my college friends, who inspired the characters, Mackenzie Bishop and Rachel Hoyt. Thank you to the real-life Mackenzie for specifically letting me make a story about our time in college.

And thank you to the real inspiration for Mike Sienkiewicz as well.

I also want to thank my grandma Marjorie Jansen for her encouragement and reading the proof. I know YA fiction isn't your thing, but I appreciate all your words of support when we were pen pals during the pandemic.

A good writer needs a great editor, and I want to thank Megan Sanders for her diligent work. *Mike* is now here because of you.

Lastly, I'd like to thank Yulia Horobets for making the epitome of gorgeous book covers. Thank you for taking my vague cover ideas and making something beautiful.

Gaby Knight is a former journalist and a current hopeless romantic existentialist. She lives in Alabama with her husband, Justin, cats, Luna and Cleo, and dog, Lassie. You can follow her on Instagram at GabyKnightAuthor.

www.ingramcontent.com/pod-product-compliance
Lightning Source LLC
Chambersburg PA
CBHW020420110726
47899CB00006B/2061